wv

A

CANDLELIGHT REGENCY SPECIAL

CANDLELIGHT REGENCIES

PASSING FANCY

Mary Linn Roby

A CANDLELIGHT REGENCY SPECIAL

Published by
Dell Publishing Co., Inc.
1 Dag Hammarskjold Plaza
New York, New York 10017

Dell ® TM 681510, Dell Publishing Co., Inc.

ISBN: 0-440-16770-1

Printed in the United States of America

First printing—March 1980

PASSING FANCY

Chapter One

~~~~~~

"I must warn you, Mrs. Capstone, that I am not at all certain Bath will suit me," the Duke of Jennings declared, allowing himself to be lowered onto a wing chair by one niece, while the other carefully raised one of his booted feet and then the other until both rested comfortably on the footstool which their landlady had thoughtfully provided.

"The waters will do you a world of good, Your Grace," that thin-nosed personage replied, inclining her head in such a subservient manner that her mob cap threatened to slip over her eyes.

"Nasty-tasting stuff, I imagine," the Duke muttered, fixing her with a penetrating aristocratic stare. "Pah! I know what to expect. Never should have let myself be talked into this. Doctors are all fools or worse. Damme, what's that noise? It's enough to raise the dead!"

"It's church bells, Uncle," Susan said a bit breathlessly, having just returned from running into one of the two bedchambers which adjoined the little sitting room to fetch a pillow to place under his head. "Surely you remember remarking on them when our coach reached the outskirts of the city?"

"Take care of me wig, gel!" the Duke roared. "You've half knocked it off my head. Get away and let your sister attend to me. She may have a sharp tongue, but she has a gentle touch."

"Calm yourself, Uncle, do," Jennifer said mildly, patting the pillow into place and reinstating the old gentleman's wig to its proper position.

"It is the custom of the city to have the church bells rung whenever visitors arrive, Your Grace," Mrs. Capstone explained.

"If that ain't a fine way of alerting every tradesman and sharpster in the place that a new victim has arrived, I never heard of one!" the Duke replied in his usual gracious manner.

"Never mind, Uncle," Jennifer murmured, unstrapping a small valise and beginning to arrange various jars and small bottles and paper packets on the table beside his chair. "It's quiet now."

The words were no sooner out of her mouth,

however, than what seemed to be a faint echo of the recent clamor was heard.

"Odd rot it, what's that?" the Duke demanded.

"It's the city waits, Your Grace," their landlady murmured apologetically. "They'll ring their bells outside the window—a sort of welcome serenade like—until they're paid. Half a guinea for a common visitor, sir, and a guinea if there's a title involved."

"What a quaint custom, Uncle!" Susan cried, hurrying to the window and peering out, blond curls dangling about her charming face.

"Highway robbery's a better name for it!" the Duke replied, his face growing narrower by the minute. "But I suppose there's no help for it. Where's that addlepated abigail of yours, Jennifer? Tell her to take this down to them and send them on their way."

"Molly's down there already!" Susan informed him excitedly. "How quick she is to set up acquaintances. Why, one of the fellows has given her a bell to ring!"

"Has he, by Jove!" the Duke blustered, struggling to get out of his chair. "That gel will be nothing but trouble for us. Take my word on it. Why, in the country there wasn't a groom or a footman safe from her! I warned you . . . "

"Do be quiet, Uncle," Jennifer said in a determined manner, pushing him back into his chair with little of the gentleness for which she had previously been acclaimed. "Dr. Haskin told you that you must keep your temper at all costs and I am determined to see to it that you do no matter how angry it makes you. Here is the guinea, Susan! Drop it down to them. And tell Molly to give over bell ringing at once and wait on us immediately."

"The gel needs a sharp word, Niece."

"And she will have more than one, Uncle," Jennifer replied, her dark eyes shining with determination. "Now, Mrs. Capstone, I think we should have a few words about my uncle's diet, for he is very particular."

The mention of diet had an immediately soothing effect on the Duke, who never felt more himself than when discussing his health, no matter how indirectly. Indeed, as he allowed himself the luxury of turning certain favored words such as "oyster patties" and "pickled salmon" over on his tongue, he fell into a droning, near-hypnotic state with which both sisters were well familiar.

"There, Mrs. Capstone," Susan whispered, edging close to their landlady and beckoning Jennifer to join her. "No need to listen, I assure you. Jennie has made out a list and besides there are so many more exciting things to talk about."

"My sister has been on pins and needles for the past few weeks," Jennifer said dryly, "for fear that we will not observe the proprieties at such a fashionable spa."

"It is only that we have led such a sheltered life in the country," Susan protested. "To be sure, Lady Tassing, whose estate borders Uncle's, wished to counsel us, but Uncle would insist on our avoiding the subject of Bath since, until the very last minute, he would not give his assurance that he would make the trip, and he said he did not wish Lady Tassing to fill our minds . . . "

"Mrs. Capstone cannot wish to hear the story of our lives, Susan," Jennifer said in a low voice. "If we have questions, we must ask them quickly, for Uncle has already mentioned syllabub a second time and will soon be coming to the end of his recitation."

"Well, Miss," the landlady said, assuming a knowledgeable expression which was only marred by the cast in one of her beady eyes, "it is usual to join the subscription library where one can borrow books and read the London newspapers, not to speak of . . . "

"Tell us of the balls, Mrs. Capstone, do!" Susan interrupted her. "The library can well wait till another time."

"Balls, Miss? Why there are two a week, one at each of the assembly houses. Formal affairs, they are. Or ought to be. Why, I declare, in the time of Mr. Nash, matters were arranged properly, with ladies taking the floor according to rank and none of the present crush, not to mention . . ."

"I expect we will need a chaperon," Susan declared. "But there is no trouble there, for Lady Tassing intends to surprise Uncle by arriving tomorrow. Indeed, Mrs. Capstone, we were charged with reserving her a room in this very house if one is available. A suite, if possible, although she is not particular, since her main interest is to be as near to us as possible."

"By that I believe she means that she wishes to be in close proximity to Uncle," Jennifer said with a touch of irony in her voice.

"Lady Tassing takes the greatest interest in Uncle's health," Susan protested.

"Indeed, she takes a greater interest than he wishes," her sister replied. "I believe my uncle would be well enough pleased, Mrs. Capstone, if you could assure us that your house is presently filled."

"Why no, Miss. I can always find room for the gentry. There is a Captain Newton who has not seen his way clear to pay for his lodgings for the past fortnight. He will be on his way tomorrow morning, I assure you."

"PLOVER'S EGGS AND A FILLET OF SALMON!" the Duke declared in a loud voice. "And if I think of any other small item, Madam, I will let you know of it."

Like one awakening from an agreeable trance, he roused himself and stared at them.

"Have you been listening closely?" he demanded of the landlady, who proceeded to shake her head and nod it as nearly simultaneously as is possible, all the while edging toward the door.

"But Uncle!" Susan exclaimed. "Let us first be given the opportunity to find out what our routine for tomorrow must be."

"First things first," the Duke assured her. "What have we here? My medicine not unpacked completely! Not to mention my books! How am I to diagnose my own symptoms if I do not have my books at hand? Damme, I knew we should have brought Jack with us! What am I to do without my man? Molly was to serve us all, you said. And now, I ask you, where is the gel? Still ringing bells, eh? Still ringing bells?"

Susan rushed to the outpost from which she had previously reported on their abigail's whereabouts.

"Molly!" she cried. "Oh dear, she is in such a close conversation with a coachman that I cannot seem to get her attention."

"Throw something at her!" the Duke roared. "Throw something solid. That set of pokers, perhaps. Ah, the jade, the jade! I told you that we should have left her at home."

"Allow me to attend to the matter, Your Grace," Mrs. Capstone said tentatively, clutching the doorknob.

"Indeed you must not leave us until we know what our routine is to be!" Susan cried.

The landlady whirled about twice in a perfect fit of indecision.

"Do let us settle our routine, Uncle," Jennifer said wearily. "After all, you have come to take the waters, and it is only suitable that we should be informed of the correct procedures."

"Procedures, procedures," the Duke grumbled. "I should have known that would be what it would come down to. Very well. No doubt that chit would be of as little use to us up here as she is below. Enlighten us as to what our absurd behavior is to be, Mrs. Capstone, and pray be quick about it for it is time for my dose of hartshorn. After that I will be ready for my supper. I believe you heard me speak of oyster patties, Madam."

"Oh yes, Your Grace!" the landlady exclaimed. "Supper will be brought up directly. As for your routine, a sedan chair will take you to Cross Bath tomorrow, if it suits your fancy."

"A bath!" the Duke exclaimed. "What have I to do with baths? Do I not appear to be suitably clean, Madam?"

"Do not tease Mrs. Capstone, Uncle," Jennifer said sternly. "You know quite well that Dr. Haskin told you in some detail about the therapeutic value of immersion in hot mineral water."

"Immersion!" the Duke grumbled. "Am I to be treated like a slab of mutton which is too tough for the table in its natural state?"

It was a rhetorical question and, as such, could properly be ignored.

"But what shall we do while Uncle is immersed, dear Mrs. Capstone?" Susan demanded.

"Why, you and your sister must visit the Pump Room, Miss," the landlady replied in a considerable dither. "One meets one's friends there."

"We have no friends in Bath," Jennifer noted.

"Then we shall make some," Susan insisted eagerly. "And when we have taken the waters, what shall we do next, Mrs. Capstone?"

"You will return here and wait for me, gel," her uncle assured her.

Susan cast him a rebellious glance.

"What will the other young ladies do?" she demanded. "After all, Uncle, when you are feeling better there will be no need of our constant attendance."

"It is customary for the ladies to stroll to one of the coffee houses," Mrs. Capstone said tentatively, one eye on the Duke and the other on the door through which she obviously pined to make an escape. "And then at midday it is the custom to attend services at the Abbey. Dinner is generally taken at three in the afternoon and then there is a pause until evening when there is card playing, not to mention plays and concerts to be attended."

"Enough of this folly!" the Duke exclaimed. "We have come to Bath for me to be cured, Madam. An unlikely prospect, I admit, but one to

15

which I intend to dedicate myself and everyone about me for a few days, at least. What is all this talk of plays and concerts?"

"Mrs. Capstone only seeks to give us a general overview, Uncle," Jessica said soothingly. "Of course our first concern will always be you and the state of your health."

"But we shall want some entertainment, Jennie!" Susan protested.

Her sister shot her a warning glance of the sort Susan knew well enough to plunge her into instant silence. Since they had been left their uncle's wards four years ago on the unfortunate deaths of their parents of diphtheria, they had learned that their main effort in life was to be the contentment of a hypochondriac who demanded little more than the concentrated attention of everyone around him. It was, as Jennifer had often warned Susan, a small enough price to pay for the security they enjoyed.

As for the future, that was in their uncle's hands and, although he had often promised each of them a coming-out in London, it was Jennifer's considered opinion that they were fortunate enough that his illnesses had led him to Bath where social strictures were relaxed and where, with any sort of good fortune at all, they would be able to enjoy the sort of social intercourse which, due to the isolation of Marsden Hall, had hitherto been denied them.

"Card playing!" the Duke continued. "Plays and concerts! Not to mention dancing, I suppose."

"Pray forget that the subject of entertainment was ever mentioned, Uncle," Jennifer said firmly. "Here. Let me set out the rest of your medicines. There is the hartshorn, you see, and the new ointment the doctor prescribed. Susan, do set yourself to unpacking Uncle's books, for you know he likes to refer to them at the moment when a new pain strikes him. That is the box, there. And now, Uncle, while we occupy ourselves, had you not better order supper?"

Thus she cleverly pacified him, making no objection to oyster patties, which Dr. Haskin had expressly forbidden, nor to a host of other delicacies. Only when he came to speak of wine did she protest.

"But you know, Uncle, that you must drink no wine, not to mention port, which will give you no end of pain in your leg tomorrow."

"Let the damned waters take care of my leg!" the Duke declared. "What am I here for, gel, if not to live my life the way I choose and have the waters care for the results? I have brought my own wine, Mrs. Capstone. I want no inferior product. My groom will have seen to the unloading of it by now, or it will go the worse for him! I hope you have a proper cellar."

"As you see, Mrs. Capstone," Jennifer said dryly, "my uncle is a gentleman who knows his

17

own mind. But we have kept you long enough, I think. There is only one other matter and that is the message that must be sent to the physician here whom Dr. Haskin recommended. Uncle, do you recollect his name?"

"Wicket, Wemscott, Wilcott," the Duke droned, his attention distracted by the books Susan was placing on the shelf close by his chair.

"That will be Dr. Welsome, Miss," Mrs. Capstone told Jennifer. "I will send Tom to fetch him at once, if you like."

"Tomorrow will be soon enough," Jennifer assured her. "For the moment my uncle's supper should be our first preoccupation for his temper stands in exact relationship to the time he has been without nourishment."

Mrs. Capstone literally fled to the door on hearing this and gave a little cry when, on opening it, she disclosed a couple in close embrace.

"Tom!" the landlady cried.

"Molly!" Jennifer exclaimed.

The red-haired abigail detached herself with a proficiency which hinted at long practice and darted into the room, but not before Mrs. Capstone was observed to be setting about Tom's ears with her fists in a distracted fashion.

"Ah, there you are, chit!" the Duke of Jennings roared. "Let me tell you this, Miss! If your behavior does not improve immediately, you will be sent back to the country! Your mother may have been my cook these many years, but I will not have such doings! Dash it, gel, do you hear me?"

"La, Your Grace, I was no more than being friendly," Molly declared, flushed-faced.

"I'm sure we all know what that means," the Duke assured her ominously.

"Molly will see to unpacking our things," Jennifer assured him. "The bedroom to the right, Molly. Yes, that is the door. Our valises are there. Susan's things are to be put in the larger cabinet. Now, run along, do. You can have supper downstairs in the kitchen when you are finished. But you must mind your ways!"

Assuming an innocent smile, Molly dropped a curtsy of such magnificent proportions as to send Susan into a fit of laughter.

"Mind you, she'll not last the week before she's in some sort of trouble," the Duke began.

"Look at your books, Uncle," Jennifer replied. "Do they not look handsome set out all together? Now, here are your spectacles. Have we forgotten anything, do you think?"

"Ah, there is my Hippocrates and my Galen," the Duke murmured contentedly as she fitted the spectacles over his ears. "And subscription journals and Cullen's *First Lines on the Practice of Physick*. Are all four volumes there? Yes, so they are. And here, if I do not mistake myself, is someone to set out the plate for supper."

While a demure little maid set out the plate and

silver on a table drawn conveniently to the Duke's side, Susan gestured her sister to the alcove formed by three long windows.

"Oh, Jennie," she whispered. "Do you see the lights! Tomorrow night we will be dancing."

"Do not set your fancy on it," Jennifer warned in a low voice. "A great deal will depend on tomorrow."

"But for the present he is happy," Susan protested. "Only see how he is smiling at the thought of oyster patties."

"It will take more than oyster patties to give us our freedom," Jennifer assured her. "Indeed, from what Mrs. Capstone has said of Bath, I am not sure I want mine, for it seems a frivolous enough place."

"But that is precisely my prescription for both of us," Susan replied happily. "We have grown dull in the country, I fancy, and a large dose of frivolity is what is needed. Oh, Jennie, I can scarcely wait for the sun to rise."

Chapter Two

Despite Susan's fine, eager words, she was the sluggard whom Jennifer had difficulty in arousing from her slumber at nine.

"Oh, do go away, Jennie, and let me sleep!" she begged, burying her golden head in one pillow and placing another over all.

Jennifer's fine dark eyes sparkled with amusement and determination for it had always pleased her to treat her younger sister as a child, a role that even now when she was eighteen seemed to suit her.

"Oh!" she cried in mock horror. "A spider, Susan! Such a great spider hanging just above your bare arm. Why, I believe he is about to drop! Yes, there he goes!"

With a scream, Susan quitted the bed and was halfway across the room before she noticed that Jennifer was laughing.

"Gunchen!" Susan cried, snatching one of the petticoats which Molly, with her usual flair for tidiness, had left draped over a chair and beating her sister about the head with it until Jennifer's dark curls were in a tangle. "You pippin! To frighten me that way!"

"It was a manner of persuading you to leave the bed," Jennifer reminded her, taking the petticoat captive. "Now, we must be very serious and you must put on your dressing gown at once and come to the sitting room window."

"But why?" Susan demanded. "What on earth could there be to see at this hour in the morning when the sun is just barely over the rooftops?"

"Uncle is off on his first visit to the baths," Jennifer told her. "Do hurry, Susan, for it is a sight worth seeing, I declare. The doctor arrived half an hour ago and was insistent. I never thought to see Uncle in the streets in dishabille, but once he was assured it was the custom . . . "

Together the two girls hurried into the sitting room where they joined Molly at the window.

"La, what a fuss the old sapskull is making!" she cried. "I mean to say, the gentleman is making such a fuss. I swear they'll never get him in the chair! He'll never fit, not he!"

The conveyance she referred to being a sedan

22

chair, which bore a marked resemblance to an upright coffin mounted on two rails and offering access by a very narrow door, Jennifer thought she might be right since her uncle's rotund proportions did not seem to lend themselves to such narrow quarters. Dr. Welsome, being a cadaverous gentleman, as suited his profession, had just managed to push the Duke inside and fit himself in as well, as his nieces elbowed the abigail aside and leaned out the window for a better view. There was only a momentary glimpse of their uncle's face, challenging his scarlet dressing gown in hue, and then the bearers, with simultaneous groans, clasped the poles, raised the chair, and started on their way.

"He's off!" Molly cried.

"That will be quite enough," Jennifer warned the abigail, disguising her own amusement with an effort. "You are not attending the races at Newmarket! And I will be well pleased if I never again hear you refer to the Duke as a sapskull."

"It's just a manner of speaking, Miss," Molly said pertly, twisting one red curl around her finger.

"And this is another way of speaking," Jennifer told her. "I will read you the sort of a scold you will not forget unless you learn to speak with more decorum. In fact I will go further than that and see that you are sent back to the country posthaste unless you mend your ways. Have I made myself quite clear?"

"But Uncle did look so funny," Susan protested. "I can quite understand why Molly forgot herself."

"Thank you, Miss," the abigail said, dropping the parody of a curtsy.

"You'll be to blame in part if Uncle decides to send her home," Jennifer warned her sister. "If it were not for the way you spoil her . . ."

"There's others would," Molly said, turning with a little flounce.

"There's others who would pretend to want the opportunity," Jennifer reminded her. "Jake, the blacksmith's son, was one if I recall correctly."

"Jake Turner was naught to me, Miss," Molly declared petulantly, at the same time having the good grace to blush.

"And a good thing it was we brought you to your senses in time," Jennifer said.

"Then there was the groom's helper!" Susan exclaimed, eagerly joining the discussion. "What was his name? Do you remember how you believed all his promises, Molly? The ones about setting you up as a fine lady in London once he'd regained the fortune that he lost . . . How *did* he lose it? I forget now. And then Uncle discovered that he was not two months out of jail for having robbed a house in Berkshire."

"It's time for my breakfast, Miss," the abigail

replied, adopting a most aristocratic swaying of the hips as she started for the door.

"Ah, but you are mistaken, Molly," Jennifer told her. "It is time for ours, I believe. See to it at once, if you please."

"Very well, Miss!" Molly declared with a wealth of defiance in her voice. "Of course there's some who wouldn't want their servant to come all over faint from lack of nourishment, but . . . "

"If you were to come over faint, lack of nourishment would not be the first thought to come to my mind," Jennifer assured her with a wicked glance at her sister, who collapsed onto the sofa in a fit of giggling.

"If your uncle was to know how indelicate you can be, Miss, he'd be that put out!" Molly retorted.

"Breakfast!" Jennifer cried, advancing on her rapidly.

Assuming an expression of the utmost displeasure, Molly departed, the effect being ruined, however, by the sound of hearty laughter and an accompanying squeal as soon as the door was closed behind her.

"Do you suppose that fellow Tom was waiting for her?" Susan demanded with wide-eyed curiosity.

"Given Molly's talents, it might be anyone," Jennifer assured her. "No. It would be beneath our dignity to peek. They've gone now, at any rate. We can only hope that she remembers why we sent her downstairs."

Molly did remember, although she took some time in returning with a laden tray, and yet it was with some alacrity that she accomplished a tidying of her young mistresses' chamber and even more haste with which she left them on the excuse that she would fetch another pot of tea from the kitchen. Clearly she meant to be brisk while she was with them and as tardy to return as possible, an attitude which did not bode well.

When Molly finally returned, without the tea but with the information that there were callers, the two girls were dressed, Jennifer in pale blue which suited her complexion and Susan in pink sprigged muslin. Before the abigail could complete her announcement, a broad-bosomed lady in puce, her forehead hidden under yellow curls of the sort not often seen on someone so long of tooth, lumbered into the room. Following close behind her was a girl whose dark beauty rivaled Jennifer's own.

"Cousin Amelia!" Susan cried, stretching out her arms. "We did not know that you and Aunt were in Bath!"

It was left to Jennifer to be engulfed by the older woman's embrace.

"Lady Ellison and Miss Amelia Ellison," Molly announced unnecessarily.

"Bring us tea, Molly," Jennifer said, struggling free from what threatened to be a suffocating encounter. Kind as her uncle's sister was, she had often wished that Lady Daphne did not find it necessary to touch and hold and fondle everyone she was fond of with such distressing enthusiasm. Indeed, she often found this a paradox, since, in other matters of social exchange, Lady Daphne preferred irony to enthusiasm. Perhaps, Jennifer thought, she was overly fond of welcoming people since each fresh encounter promised a new disillusionment to follow.

"Delightful to see you!" Amelia murmured, planting a dry kiss on Jennifer's cheek since, unlike her mother, exuberance was not her strongest suit. "When Mama received Uncle's letter, she said that we must call on you at once, even though it did mean we could not attend the Pump Room this morning."

A certain malevolence in Amelia's blue eyes gave Jennifer to understand that her cousin did not expect kinship to make such extraordinary demands on her a second time.

"Of course," the girl continued, "there is still time for all of us to attend. Our carriage is waiting, and you and Susan need not worry about your gowns, for anything is allowed in the morning."

The stylishness of her own pale green silk costume, with the yards of lace fringing the square

27

neck and three-quarter sleeves, added to the insult implicit in her suggestion, but Jennifer, accustomed as she was to Amelia's manner, shrugged it away.

"I am afraid that Uncle will expect to find us here when he returns from his first visit to the baths," she said. "So sorry to have caused you to miss a morning of flirtation, Cousin."

"Now, you two must not resort to nit-picking at one another!" Lady Daphne exclaimed. "I will not have it, do you hear? Amelia does not at all mind missing her few hours at the Pump Room, although she would like to have you think so, for she has all manner of conquests to brag about and you both know nothing suits her better than a good boast."

"Mama!" Amelia cried in some displeasure.

"Come, let us sit down," Lady Daphne continued resolutely, "and I will say the usual things. How charming you both look! And what a pleasant apartment! I trust my brother is in his usual ill humor! Indeed, I cannot believe that he allowed himself to be persuaded to come to a place which may actually relieve him of some of his complaints. And do you really mean that he is at this very moment at the baths? He must be at the Cross, for the Queen's is only for ladies. I wonder what he will say when he finds himself immersed in water with members of the opposite sex?"

Her laughter was robust and filled the room, or

that part of it which she did not already occupy.

"But I thought you said that the Queen's Bath was for ladies, Aunt!" Susan cried.

"There are all sorts of ladies, my dear," Lady Daphne replied, tapping her nose with one finger. "And there are a good many who prefer to take their treatment in the company of gentlemen. I understand it is all very informal, if you take my meaning."

"I declare I do not take it very clearly," Jennifer told her.

"Well, it is all very well for the gentlemen's modesty," Lady Daphne said cheerfully, "for they are helped into canvas drawers and waistcoats by an attendant. But the capacious dresses provided for the ladies quickly fill with water, or so I am told, and at times the limits of propriety are exceeded, I believe, with no one taking exception. Bath is such a free and easy place. Is it not, Amelia?"

"There is certainly a good deal to occupy one's attention," her daughter replied in a self-satisfied manner. "Particularly if one is young and pretty. Why, last night at the Assembly House : . ."

"But what must Uncle be thinking?" Jennifer interrupted her. "He will be certain he is in a den of iniquity."

"I have often thought that a den of iniquity would be a perfect place for Alfred," Lady Daphne said reflectively. "He is such a sapskull

29

about so many things, and has been since he was a boy."

"Why, that is exactly what Molly said!" Susan exclaimed.

Jennifer silenced her with a glance.

"But surely, Aunt, you do not mean that there will be—improprieties."

"I would be surprised if there were not," Lady Daphne assured her cheerfully. "But he will be in good hands. There are attendants who keep everyone upright. At least everyone who wishes to be. And there are certain little touches. For example, each lady has her own little floating dish in which she places her handkerchief and perhaps a nosegay. No doubt Alfred will be quite charmed."

"I find that most unlikely," Jennifer said glumly. "But never mind. Here is Molly with the tea. Will you have a cup, Aunt? Amelia? Cream or sugar or both? Yes, Molly. Do take the breakfast things away. And please be on call if we should want you further."

"Pardon me, Miss, but there being a tear in your yellow taffeta, I thought I might just hurry to one of the shops and find some matching thread," the abigail replied, making such a rapid retreat that Jennifer did not have time to stop her.

"I suppose that is the last we shall see of her this morning," Susan said, smiling.

"It may be the last we see of her all day," Jennifer said grimly.

"She is a natural flirt," Lady Daphne declared. "I have often said as much to Alfred. 'Give her her head,' I tell him, but he feels such an obligation to protect her, her mother having been his cook these many years. 'There are some that must be given their own way,' I've told him often enough. And who should know better than I," she added with a meaningful glance at her daughter, who seemed not in the least disconcerted.

"If you are referring to me, Mama," Amelia said, "I think you must agree that my way is always reasonable. Why, most of the young ladies whom I know are all too willing to allow their heads to be turned by a handsome face or, even worse, a uniform."

"And some, no doubt, go so far as to concern themselves with a gentleman's character," Jennifer said dryly, knowing as she did something of her cousin's ambitions.

"I admire those who sit well on a horse!" Susan exclaimed. "And courage! That is something I cannot resist. I wish it were still the fashion for gentlemen to wear their swords. And use them, too. What a shame it is that duels now must be such hole-in-the-corner affairs. Why, I think the law never should have been turned against them!"

"It was in Bath that they were first banned," Amelia said in a pedantic manner. "I know something of the history of the place, you see, for I always believe that it is a great encouragement to conversation, if one can speak of something beside the superficial give-and-take which characterizes most conversations here."

"Indeed, she can show herself to good account in history and literature, and is presently doing what she can to acquire a working repertoire of philosophical terms, although I believe that is rather difficult." Lady Daphne smiled in a strange way. "Of course," she added, "it is unlikely whether she will meet many philosophers at the Pump Room, but Amelia likes to be prepared. I believe that of all her little stores of knowledge, the history of Bath has been most successful."

"Why must you forever mock me, Mama?" Amelia demanded. "I was only about to explain to Susan that Beau Nash, of whom she must have heard, since he was for so long Master of Ceremonies at the Assembly Rooms here, long since decided that dueling should be discouraged and it was not long before it became *comme il faut* for swords to be displayed, let alone used."

"Did Mr. Nash support cowardice then?" Susan demanded.

"On the contrary," Amelia said, "he took great pains to prove his own manhood before he imposed the ban. I have it on excellent authority that when he overheard a gentleman commenting in an uncouth manner on the charms of Mrs. Nash while she was in one of the baths, he pushed the fellow into the water and fought a duel with him afterward, which he won, although no one was much hurt."

"A halfhearted affair, from what I hear," her mother murmured, and was ignored.

"Mr. Nash made his point," Amelia went on. "And then, of course, he was free to publish his ban and swords disappeared."

"That was over sixty years ago," Lady Daphne said, "and all was accomplished with the assistance of the city authorities. I find it difficult to understand, my dear, why you persist in giving so much admiration to a man who started his career as a professional gambler."

"It is thanks to Beau Nash that gambling is conducted with decorum here," Amelia replied. "No one dared defy him."

"Now, if you will be a historian, you must be accurate," Lady Daphne retorted with some little annoyance. "I can remember my mother telling me that Lord Peterborough was often seen wearing his riding boots in the Assembly Hall even though Nash had placed a ban on them."

"Everyone who knows anything about the history of Bath knows that Lord Peterborough was an eccentric, Mama!" Amelia explained impatiently. "Why I have read that he did his own marketing of a morning. Fancy, he would wear his blue ribbon and star of the Garter and allow himself to be seen with a chicken under one arm and carrots and cabbages under the other."

"We were discussing what some young ladies found engaging in gentlemen," Jennifer reminded them, for she had listened to such quibbling between mother and daughter before and found it tiring, since she had never known either to win and was aware that, given the opportunity, they would not give up a debate of this sort until more had been said on the subject than anyone could wish to hear.

"Indeed we were!" Susan cried. "What is it that appeals to *you*, Amelia, if it is neither looks nor character nor courage?"

"I think our cousin dotes on power," Jennifer suggested. "What she said about Beau Nash indicated something of the sort."

"Precisely so," Amelia replied. "You *are* perceptive, Jennie. Although there is more to it than that."

"I expect that wealth is a prerequisite," Jennifer murmured.

"Exactly!" Amelia exclaimed.

"And high rank?"

"The highest possible!"

"But character may go by the board?"

"I find it does not interest me unduly."

"And courage is beside the point?"

"A gentleman with power, wealth, and rank may well dispense with courage, I believe."

"Appearance does not concern you, either?"

"Within limits," Amelia replied.

"You will not be difficult to satisfy then," Jennifer concluded, "for I have heard that Bath abounds with just the sort of person you have so aptly described."

"Indeed it does!" Amelia told her. "I have been busy since I came here making lists."

"She rates them as one might rank horses at Newmarket," Lady Daphne said. "At the present, I believe an Earl who is all of seventy and gouty to boot is the favorite."

"It is just as I said, Mama," Amelia pouted. "You make a mockery of everything. Of course, he has been most attentive, but a match between us is unthinkable. Everyone would imagine that I married him for . . . "

"Power, wealth, and rank?" Jennifer suggested.

"Oh, you are too bad, all of you!" her cousin cried. "I do my best to be practical and all the thanks I receive in return . . . "

She broke off as a knock sounded on the door and in a moment Lady Tassing was among them, darting like a faded butterfly from one to the other, dropping kisses on foreheads and cheeks, all the time uttering little cries of delight.

"Everything is arranged!" she announced finally, coming to a halt in the very center of the room, a tiny person dressed in a neat gray traveling costume and wearing a jaunty bonnet from which an ostrich feather sprouted. "I have spoken with Mrs. Capstone and I am to have a suite. My luggage will be removed there as soon as a certain Captain Newton has been convinced to quit the rooms. In the meantime I will make myself quite cozy here. Dear Lady Daphne! Dear Amelia! Dear Jennifer! And dear, dear Susan! And where is the Duke? If you only knew how I have looked forward to surprising him!"

There was no time for anyone to answer, since the door opened again immediately and a harassed gentleman whom Jennifer could only assume was Dr. Welsome appeared with her uncle following close behind, scowling and muttering, an attitude which she put down to an unfortunate experience at the baths until she saw that his right hand gripped Molly's wrist and that the abigail was being dragged with very little formality into the room.

"Far enough, Welsome! Far enough!" the Duke declared. "Safe and sound! Thank ye and good-bye! As for you, trollop, you can explain what you were doing loitering with that young scoundrel by the front door."

"But Your Grace!" Molly exclaimed. "That was the greengrocer's boy and we were only discussing the price of spring peas in a friendly fashion. Besides, you do not want to bother your head about that now. Only look! You have company, sir."

The Duke of Jennings raised his head on which his periwig was set precariously. His face was flushed and his scarlet dressing gown was crumpled.

"Damme!" he exclaimed. "Daphne, is it you? And Amelia. And . . . but it cannot be!"

"I have too much concern for your welfare to remain in the country, sir," Lady Tassing announced, flitting toward him.

"Stand back!" the Duke declared, raising both hands against her. "Stand back, I say! I can tolerate only so much in any day! Support me to my chamber, chit, and close the door. Jack must be sent for at once. In these past two hours I have suffered more female associates than can be endured by someone in my condition. Hussies, all of them, lolling about in the same water as . . . "

Still muttering, he retired, and Molly faced the company with an expression of delight.

"Bath is such a lovely place!" she cried. "I declare, I could stay here forever!"

"I must see to Uncle's medicine," Jennifer murmured.

"And I will choose one of his medical journals to comfort him," Susan said.

"I think Mama and I may as well make an appearance at the Pump Room," Amelia suggested.

"Poor Alfred never could deal with reality," Lady Daphne murmured, rising.

"I will remain and dedicate myself to his recovery," Lady Tassing announced. "The dear, courageous man!"

"Hypochondriac!" Lady Daphne exclaimed.

"Tyrant!" Amelia exclaimed. "Dear Uncle has always been so tiresome."

"A sapskull," Molly could be heard to murmur. "But what do I care as long as we stay here in Bath! And stay we must!"

Chapter Three

==

With the arrival of Jack from Marsden Hall that
very evening, Susan and Jennifer found themselves relieved of a good many of the irksome duties surrounding the care of their uncle which
would have kept them from the Pump or the Assembly Rooms. With his usual good nature, the
Duke of Jennings's man, a sprightly fellow of
middle age who had been trained by his father,
who had been the Duke's valet before him, took
charge of his master with a sure hand and a
smooth tongue, making him as comfortable as anyone could have done and convincing him that,
despite his violent response to his first visit to the
baths, he should return to them in the morning.

Thus it was that the two girls visited the Pump

Room in the company of Lady Daphne and Amelia, Lady Tassing having indicated a desire to remain at their lodging house to await the Duke's return from his second immersion.

"After all, my dear," she reminded Jennifer blithely, "I did not come to Bath to be entertained. Your uncle and I will have a little chat about his health. You know as well as I how much that will please him."

Jennifer knew all too well, for she had often observed her uncle to perform the most unusual maneuvers to avoid Lady Tassing when she arrived at Marsden Hall for her daily visit, cleverly arranging it so that she never put in an appearance at the same time, all the better to take the Duke unawares.

"I am determined to be as neighborly here as I ever was in the country," Lady Tassing declared in her usual forthright manner. "Now, you and Susan must be off to enjoy yourselves. Pray put your uncle out of your mind."

And that, Jennifer found, was extraordinarily easy to do for, although she was not as exhilarated by her first exposure to the society of Bath as was Susan, she found much to admire in the elegance of the Palladian architecture and even more to distract her in the crowded streets. Any concern she had had about Susan and her simple sprigged-muslin gowns was dispelled by the dishabille of those members of the *haut ton* who stood about the

Pump Room, gossiping and sipping the water which was so evil-tasting that Jennifer was certain it must either kill or cure.

Afterward Lady Daphne introduced her nieces to a variety of people whose names Jennifer found she was at a loss to remember later. They then left the crush and took themselves to one of the many coffee houses nearby where more introductions were performed, and were subsequently returned to the house on Gay Street, having paused on the way to make their two-guinea subscription to the Assembly Rooms.

"Tonight we will attend the upper room," Amelia announced as their carriage was drawn to a halt before their lodging house in front of which Molly was engaged in a spirited exchange with a handsome young footman in green and silver livery.

"Your abigail has considerable good taste," Lady Daphne said dryly as the two girls stepped to the ground. "If I am not mistaken that is one of Lord Burton's servants, and everyone knows that Lord Burton is most particular."

"I intend to speak to her," Jennifer said grimly.

"It will be a waste of words, I imagine," Lady Daphne replied. "Are you quite certain that you will not join us at the Abbey church at midday? A tiresome custom, in my opinion, since I have always found attendance on a Sunday quite enough and more, but on a weekday it provides another meeting place, you see, and given Amelia's determination to . . . "

"Mama!" the girl exclaimed, flushing in the most attractive manner possible.

"I believe we have been social enough for one day," Jennifer replied, distracted by Molly's giggles.

"But we *will* go to the ball tonight, will we not, Jennie?" Susan demanded.

"If Uncle sees fit to permit it," Jennifer replied, nodding good-bye to her aunt and cousin and proceeding, with a pinch, a prod, and a whisper, to convince Molly to enter the house with them.

Jennifer was prevented from reading the abigail the scold she deserved as soon as she would have liked, however, for Mrs. Capstone was waiting in the hallway to make some inquiries concerning the dinner to be served at three, which was, she assured Jennifer, the hour reserved for the taking of such nourishment at Bath. By the time the menu had been approved, Molly and Susan had disappeared. Mounting the stairs, Jennifer found Lady Tassing at the door of their rooms, taking her leave after what had apparently been such a prolonged chat with the Duke that he could be seen sitting as stiffly in his chair as though he had been turned to stone, his broad, red face set in an expression of profound dismay.

"My dear!" Lady Tassing cried as she met Jennifer in the doorway. "I was just this very moment telling your sister that it is all arranged. You are both to accompany me to the ball this evening. It took a bit of persuasion on my part, I assure you, but your uncle agreed at last."

"Damn the woman!" the Duke grumbled as soon as the door had closed behind her. "I would have agreed to anything to have her gone! There seems to be no end to her curiosity about my health."

"Perhaps she knows that it is a subject very close to your heart, Uncle," Jennifer suggested wickedly. "Never mind. There will be salmon for dinner."

Fortunately, the salmon was fresh. That and the other delicacies the Duke consumed, not to mention a bottle of claret, were sufficient to induce him to take a nap from which he was just awakening when Susan and Jennifer took their leave.

"Ah, my dears, you do look charming," Lady Tassing declared as they paused in the landing. "Although I wish your uncle had allowed me to give you a bit more advice as to the latest fashions before you left the country. But never mind. You have both puffed your hair quite correctly at the sides, although another time perhaps a bit of powder . . . "

Lady Tassing herself was quite à la mode in a gown cut in the latest Empire fashion with a deep bodice and high waist. Her turban was of the same shade of Parma violet and featured a diamond clip which matched the glittering jewels on her ears. Her tiny feet were displayed to advantage in slippers with heels so high as to lend several inches to her height, and it was clear from the pert way in which she carried herself that she was well pleased with her appearance.

"A hired carriage is waiting," she told the two girls, "but perhaps I might pause just long enough to look in on your uncle."

It was with some difficulty that Jennifer dissuaded Lady Tassing from this notion, and not long after they were entering the Assembly Room, which glittered with candlelight and resounded with laughter and music.

"Oh, Jennie, we do look so countrified!" Susan exclaimed as they joined the crowd that was watching the dancers bend and sway in a waltz. "Our bodices are not cut low enough and . . ."

"Look! There is Cousin Amelia!" Jennifer said, hoping to distract her sister who, no matter how out of fashion, looked a perfect picture with her blond curls fringing her forehead and her yellow, flowered brocade gown lending a touch of gold to her fair skin.

"Why, I believe she is wearing Paris net!" Susan cried. "And her cheeks are so pink. I wonder if she uses vermilion. I would not think Aunt would allow it!"

"I expect she could not prevent it, even if she tried," Jennifer replied.

44

"A fine girl like that should be given her head," Lady Tassing said. "As should you all. I know that I was given my own way when I was her age, and I have never regretted it, although it was unfair of Arthur to die so soon after we were married. I was telling your uncle only this morning that he must take a special regard for his health because . . . Ah, Lady Warrender! How pleasant to see you again. Why, we have not seen one another since the last Season in London. Allow me to present my two young friends. Miss Susan Damion. Miss Jennifer Damion. And this must be your son, Sir Edward. What a fine young man he has become. How does it come about you are not dancing, sir?"

Jennifer could not but admire the deft manner in which Lady Tassing soon arranged for Susan to take the floor with Sir Edward, but it came as a surprise to her to find herself being introduced in just such an abrupt manner to a bland-faced youth whose name she did not catch and with whom she was left, Lady Tassing archly suggesting that they must have a great deal to talk about.

"I must apologize for her ladyship," Jennifer said. "Apparently she takes her responsibilities as chaperone less seriously than I had supposed."

"Oh, it is all very free and easy here in Bath," the young gentleman replied. "Not at all like London."

"Still," Jennifer said with a smile, "there are

45

certain proprieties to be observed, and Lady Tassing mentioned your name so rapidly . . . "

"I believe she called me Sir George Billary," her companion replied, blushing like a boy. "Actually I am the Earl of Watching, although I find it difficult to believe."

"Now that is an interesting comment, indeed," Jennifer said as, of one accord, they moved away from the dance floor toward the quiet of a window alcove. "I have never found my own identity a matter of curiosity."

"I expect, Miss Damion," Lord Watching said awkwardly, "that is because you have not recently changed your station in life, as I have."

"No, I have not," Jennifer said, genuinely intrigued. "I would be glad of an explanation."

"Well, it is only this," Lord Watching replied. "An Earl is a grand title indeed, and I did not ever think to hold it, but it has happened that my uncle—not ten years older than myself, you understand—was recently killed on the Continent. He was one of Wellington's officers. Held a commission, you know. Not a professional soldier. But from what I've been given to understand, he wanted to give his services to hold 'Boney' in line. Dashed brave fellow, I hear. The thing is, he's dead and I'm an Earl, which seems a bit unfair since I never did anything to deserve it and he . . ."

Lord Watching broke off in confusion.

"So you are not as well pleased as one would think," Jennifer said thoughtfully.

"Indeed I am not, Miss Damion," the young man declared earnestly. "My uncle was a paragon, I believe. I never met him, you understand. When I was younger I believed it was because he preferred the country and my parents the city. Only just before my father's death did I discover that there had been some quarrel in the past which kept them separate."

"I would have thought that simple curiosity would have caused you to make your uncle's acquaintance once your parents were gone," Jennifer said.

"I like your forthrightness, Miss Damion," Lord Watching replied. "I would not find it so easy to confess to anyone else that I am, above all, a coward. I did not know how he would greet me if I were to ride north to his estate. Indeed, I hesitated even to send a letter, fearing that the answer might be rude. Now I expect you despise me, do you not?"

"I am sorry for you," Jennifer told him, "and that is quite a different thing. And I am glad that you feel you can confide in me. Sometimes a stranger serves where friends cannot."

"As for friends," Lord Watching told her, "I have very few of them. Many acquaintances, you understand, but few friends."

"Then you must determine to make them," Jennifer said stoutly. "You must gain confidence in yourself. You praise your uncle too fulsomely, I expect. Tell me, since you never met him, how can you be certain he was a paragon?"

"Why, everyone who knew him tells me that he was," Lord Watching said nervously. "I wonder if we should sit and talk like this. I am certain that the lady who introduced us intended we should dance."

"If that were the case, she should not have left us with the suggestion that we must have a good deal to say to one another," Jennifer replied.

"There is something in that," Lord Watching admitted. "Indeed, I am just as glad not to join the group on the floor, for I am at best an indifferent dancer."

"Then let us sit here on this window seat and talk," Jennifer urged, for although this earnest young man excited no romantic interest in her, he had kindled a spark of curiosity, since how could it be that someone so favored with title and apparent wealth could speak of himself in such a condescending fashion? They had not spoken together for five minutes yet, but she already knew that he did not consider himself a match on his uncle, that he had few friends and no one to confide in, and that he believed he cut a poor figure on the dance floor.

"I confess that I would be thankful of the opportunity to ramble on a bit," Lord Watching told her. "It is a lonely matter to be an Earl, you see. People tend to bow and scrape, you know. And then one becomes suspicious of everyone. At least I know I am beginning to feel that way. When I only had a simple Bart. after my name, very few Mamas paid me their attention. But since I have arrived in Bath . . . "

He glanced around the room nervously and, following his eyes, Jennifer found she could not blame him since more than one older woman was eyeing him speculatively, while several others were speaking seriously to their daughters and pointing fans in his direction.

"The moment we stop talking, they will descend," Lord Watching said wistfully. "It may be that they will not even wait until our tête-à-tête is over."

"I was thrown in your direction in much the same manner they would throw their daughters," Jennifer reminded him.

"Yes, but there was this," the young Earl said seriously, "the lady believed me to be someone other than I am, and that makes all the difference. Besides, Miss Damion, you will pardon me when I say I find you sympathetic."

"There is nothing for me to sympathize with," Jennie told him. "All the good fortune in the world is yours, and yet you seem unhappy. It is

49

simply that I am curious as to why that should be, for paradoxes fascinate me."

"Why, I do not believe I have thought it out carefully as yet," he told her earnestly. "I was in London when I heard the news, you see. My uncle's solicitor called me to his office. I came to see him Matthew Fuller, Bart. and left an hour later the Earl of Watching with an estate in Yorkshire and a fine house in town and I know not what else."

"Your family must have been well pleased," Jennifer suggested, since it was clear that although he wished to continue, he was not certain of the direction he should take.

"I have no family," Lord Watching told her. "I was an only child and my parents are dead. They never thought I would succeed to the title, you understand, since, as I have said, my uncle was a young man and expected to marry and raise a family of his own."

"Your friends, then," Jennifer suggested. "But then you said . . . "

"I said I had none," Lord Watching declared, "and that is the fault of the title. As soon as word got about—as it soon did, despite the fact I did not spread it—I found I was to be treated differently. People were quick to give advice and ask for assistance of a sort I would never have been asked to give when I was simply Matthew Fuller. And then I was expected to leave my bachelor apartments in St. James, where I had been comfortable enough, and move into the house on Park Lane. My uncle's house, although I believe he was rarely there except when he was forced to come to London on business. Suddenly I was besieged with invitations."

He paused again and shook his head like a bewildered boy.

"Did you not go to Yorkshire to see to your estate?" Jennifer asked him, finding his story more fascinating than the latest novel by Mrs. Radcliffe.

"Oh, yes, I went. As much to escape London as anything else, for I know nothing of country matters."

"And there you found . . ."

"A cold welcome, at best," he told her sadly. "Not that I should not have expected it. The servants were dedicated to my uncle, you see. Shea Hall was where he made his home and where he farmed the lands in earnest and saw to the welfare of his tenants. No one needed to take more than a look at me to realize I would be a poor substitute."

"You think too poorly of yourself, sir," Jennifer said encouragingly.

"Why, I could not even talk to the estate agent sensibly," he told her. "It seems that my uncle was in the way of experimenting with all manner of modern farming methods when he was called to the front. The agent seemed a very able chap and I could not blame him for growing impatient with me when it became clear that I knew nothing of agriculture."

The music and the laughter from the ballroom reached a crescendo and marked so great a contrast with Lord Watching's sad demeanor that Jennifer was hard pressed not to take his hand as a gesture of comfort. Seldom, she thought, had she seen anyone as vulnerable.

"And so you came to Bath," she murmured.

"It seemed the best thing," he told her. "There is such a crush here, so many people from so many walks of life. I thought perhaps I could go unnoticed for a while here, until I could decide what best to do."

"It must have come as a relief to you when Lady Tassing took you for someone else," Jennifer said, hoping to cheer him.

"It was a fortunate mistake," Lord Watching replied, smiling for the first time since they had met. "How else would I have made your acquaintance, Miss Damion?"

"At least I have kept you from the vultures," she replied lightly, glancing at the fond Mamas who still lurked about, waiting for their chance.

"I could not keep my identity secret," he said apologetically. "At first I was tempted, but it seemed the coward's way. Besides, there were those down from London who recognized me on my first visit to the Pump Room on my first morning here."

Jennifer nodded understandingly. "It could only have been a matter of minutes before everyone was speaking of the new Earl," she said.

"Exactly so. You are so sensible, Miss Damion. I cannot tell you what a relief it has been to me to speak openly of my problems. It puts them in perspective. Is it possible that if I were properly introduced to Lady Tassing you might consider walking with me tomorrow on the Crescent?"

"I think an introduction might be arranged," Jennifer told him. "Indeed, I believe I see Lady Tassing trying to make her way toward us now. No doubt she has realized her mistake."

"Will she be angry with me for having taken advantage of it?" Lord Watching inquired anxiously.

"Oh, no. I think not," Jennifer replied. "Indeed, I believe you will like one another well enough."

"Then I will call on you tomorrow, Miss Damion? Let us arrange it before we are interrupted."

"Perhaps it would be best if we were to meet on the Crescent at ten," Jennifer said quickly. "My uncle, who is my guardian, is ill, you see, or fancies himself so, and is not at his best when he returns from the baths as he is sure to do at about that hour. But I will tell you about him another time, if only to prove that we all have a cross to bear."

The smile she turned on Lady Tassing, who was now approaching them in her usual darting manner, changed to one of consternation as she saw that her friend carried in her wake Lady Daphne and Amelia, it being all too clear from the look in Amelia's lovely eyes that she had already been apprised of Lord Watching's true identity.

In what innocence did her companion stand! With what trepidation did Jennifer perform the necessary introductions! With what skill did Amelia ply her charms! It was only a matter of minutes before Lord Watching was being carried off to the dance floor with a bemused expression on his face.

"Amelia will need to make some changes in her list tonight," Lady Daphne remarked dryly. "How unkind of her, my dear, to walk away with your prize."

"He was not my prize," Jennifer assured her aunt grimly, "and if I can do anything to prevent it, he will not be Amelia's either."

"If you *can* keep her from adding him to her list, you will rise even higher in my estimation than you already stand," her aunt assured her, "for he seems too pleasant and unassuming a young gentleman to be able to deal with my daughter by himself."

"From what I have seen of him, he could not protect himself against Amelia for one minute," Jennifer declared, only to be interrupted by Lady Tassing.

"There, there, my dear," her ladyship announced, "there is no need for you to be out of temper, for here is someone who has asked expressly for an introduction to you. Let me present Sir John Evans. I knew his mother well."

Chapter Four

"You *are* Sir John Evans then," Jennifer said as they stood at the edge of the dance floor, waiting for the set to begin.

For a moment he looked startled as he stared down at her. Sir John was a handsome man with thick dark hair and darker eyes set deep in a fine-boned face. Erect of bearing, despite his considerable height, he wore his gray cutaway coat with the flair of a broad-shouldered man who enjoys the services of an excellent tailor. His waistcoat was discreetly embroidered and his cravat expertly arranged, although with none of the extravagance of a Macaroni.

"And may I ask why you should think I am not Sir John Evans, Miss Damion?" he inquired, raising his thick eyebrows. "Does Lady Tassing make a habit of introducing you to gentlemen who are incognito?"

"She has done so once this evening," Jennifer told him, "and I thought perhaps it could have happened again when I saw your apparent astonishment on her declaring that she knew your mother well."

He laughed.

"You are astute at reading expressions," he told her. "I did not think I had given myself away."

"I think that is a remark which needs some explanation," Jennifer replied as the musicians began tuning their instruments.

Indeed, although she sought to hide it under a display of coolness, she found herself flustered to have been placed so suddenly in the company of someone who was obviously so much a man of the world. It had been quite one thing to listen sympathetically to the Earl of Watching, who, she noticed, was standing on the opposite side of the floor listening intently to Amelia's chatter. But it was quite another matter to feel she must be clever, although why Sir John Evans should make her aware of this necessity she was not sure, unless it was the quick intelligence in his dark eyes.

"I only mean that it is true that I was taken aback when her ladyship said she knew my mother well," he replied. "I thought it best not to take issue with her, but the fact is that when I first presented myself to her, that was her first remark."

"Is it an impossibility?" Jennifer inquired. "I mean to say, Lady Tassing has always prided herself on knowing every member of the *ton*, and spends each Season in London to renew acquaintances."

"Indeed, that was what first disquieted me," Sir John Evans replied with a wry smile. "She spoke of an agreeable tête-à-tête with my mother at some great house or other only last month, and, as you suggested, that is indeed an impossibility since, unhappily, my mother has been dead these past fifteen years."

"I am sorry to hear it," Jennifer assured him. "But it was kind of you not to make mention of the fact. I believe it may be that Lady Tassing is in need of spectacles, for I have noticed certain signs of late, the most recent being that she introduced a certain gentleman to me earlier this evening as Sir George Billary, whereas it turned out that he was someone else entirely."

Sir John showed interest.

"That must have proved an embarrassment for you both," he suggested.

"On the contrary, we found it amusing," Jennifer replied. "But you will understand why I was interested to know if she had made the same sort of error a second time."

"Quite understandable," Sir John replied with

an engaging smile which somehow did not reach his eyes. "Was it that gentleman I saw you talking to so earnestly? He seems somehow familiar, but I cannot recall the name."

"It does not matter," Jennifer said quickly, remembering the Earl of Watching's reluctance to have his identity spread about. "The important thing is that Lady Tassing did not misrepresent you."

"She could scarcely have done so," Sir John assured her, "since it was I who introduced myself to her. To my certain knowledge, she and I have never met before."

"And do you make a habit of presenting yourself to ladies of a certain age quite willy-nilly, sir?" Jennifer retorted, wishing that the music would start at once since there was something about this conversation which made her uneasy. At the same time, she was eager to be free to detach Amelia from Lord Watching before he was caught entirely in her cousin's trap.

"I presented myself with the purpose of being introduced to you, Miss Damion," Sir John assured her. "I saw you enter the Assembly Room in Lady Tassing's company, you understand. I hope you are not shocked, but I assure you such manipulations are quite common here where so many strangers are, of necessity, thrown together."

There was no opportunity for Jennifer to make a reply, for just then the orchestra struck up a tune and in a moment she was being passed down the line in a contra dance of the sort she had often taken part in at home in the country and which she enjoyed quite out of reason, so much so that at the end she was left quite out of breath, which caused Sir John to suggest that a glass of punch might be in order.

A quick glance around the crowded room assured Jennifer that neither Amelia nor the Earl of Watching were in sight and, fearing the worst but acknowledging her inability to do anything about it, she took her companion's arm, the crush about the refreshment table being so great that she found it necessary to cling to him, all the while keeping a lookout for her cousin.

"And now," Sir John declared, having filled two glases with some difficulty, "let us find a quiet place to talk, for I can see that something is troubling you, Miss Damion. I only hope it is not my company."

"Indeed it is not," Jennifer assured him once they had reached the relative quiet of one of the anterooms.

"Then perhaps I may be of some assistance," he suggested.

"Oh, it is of no matter," Jennifer declared, scanning the sea of faces which drifted past the door to the main room. It had occurred to her that she could do little to thwart Amelia even if she could find her, and that was a frustration indeed. Either she could remain with this gentleman whom she found agreeable enough, or she could insist on being returned to Lady Tassing. Clearly what she could not do was to roam the Assembly Room alone, looking for Amelia and Lord Watching. Even were she to do so and to find them, what could she say to make any difference? She had promised him no dance, only a walk on the Crescent tomorrow. And by tomorrow, knowing her cousin as she did, it might be too late. Clearly the young man was in a vulnerable mood, eager to confide his problems, and there was no doubt in Jennifer's mind that Amelia could make herself as sympathetic a listener and more than she herself had been.

"A penny for your thoughts, Miss Damion," Sir John murmured, and she saw that he was staring at her thoughtfully, his dark eyes hooded.

"I was thinking of someone quite unscrupulous," Jennifer said involuntarily.

"A variety I know all too well," he assured her.

"Then perhaps you will give me your advice, sir."

"Of a certainty."

"How is it that one deals with people lacking scruples, do you think?"

For a moment his face seemed to darken.

"The answer is simplicity itself," he said in a low voice. "One must be unscrupulous in turn."

"But what if one does not know how to begin?"

"Then one should ask for assistance," he told her. "No need to name names. You have a friend, perhaps . . ."

"Yes, that is it," Jennifer declared. "I have a friend. A very new friend."

"The best sort."

For a moment she was distracted.

"How so, sir?"

"Why, with new friends we may retain our illusions," he replied. "We may think the best of them for lack of knowing the worst."

"You would make a joke of my concern, sir?"

"On the contrary, Miss Damion, I am quite serious. Do not let me distract you. You have a new friend . . ."

"Someone who is—who is quite an innocent," Jennifer replied. "Someone who is unhappy and confused."

"In a word, just of the sort to attract the unscrupulous en masse?"

"Yes. That is it exactly. Even worse, this—this person has attracted the attention of someone who is sure to lay the sort of trap for them which cannot be resisted."

"And what sort of trap is that, pray?"

He was smiling, but the expression in his eyes told her that he was taking what she said quite seriously.

"The trap of beauty, matched with charm and determination," she replied in a low voice.

"Ah, now the matter is a bit clearer," he replied. "You mention beauty, and so I must assume that the person who has set the trap is a lady."

Jennifer, who had not meant to say as much, could only nod her head.

"And it must follow that her victim is a gentleman. An innocent gentleman. I declare she has found herself a prize, for there are not many such. Come now. You disclose no confidence since you have named no names. Broad generalities will go. Has he a title?"

"He has, sir."

"And wealth?"

"Great wealth, I am afraid."

"Do not tell me that you are speaking of your uncle, Miss Damion!"

"My uncle!" Jennifer exclaimed. "Why, how could you think such a thing, sir?"

"He is the Duke of Jennings, is he not? Lady Tassing mentioned it in passing. And added that he was a great care to you."

Jennifer found herself laughing. Indeed, she laughed until the tears rolled down her cheeks.

"I am glad to have amused you," Sir John murmured.

"It is only that I have never thought of Uncle as an innocent," she told him. "Although perhaps you are right. Indeed, there is a great deal of the child about him. But as for charm and beauty mattering a whit . . ."

"I see that I have guessed incorrectly," Sir John Evans replied. "Perhaps I could be of more assistance to you if you were to speak directly."

For a moment their eyes met. And his gaze was so direct that Jennifer made her decision. After all, he was a stranger. And yet a man of the world. Who else had she to help her? Susan would be of no help at all, and Lady Daphne had long since given the rein to Amelia. As for Lady Tassing, had she not said only this evening that young ladies of determination must be given their head?

"The friend I spoke of is a certain gentleman who has recently and quite unexpectedly become an Earl," she said in a low voice. "I tell you this in confidence, sir. I cannot be more specific."

"There is no need," Sir John assured her. "An Earldom must be a heavy burden indeed."

"My friend finds it so," Jennifer replied. "He is young and inexperienced and yet he is the heir of one who is—who was a paragon of virtue."

"As for myself, I have never cared for paragons," Sir John replied. "But never mind. The gentleman you speak of must be sorely troubled. It is a sad thing to find oneself in an alien world."

"How well you have put it!" Jennifer exclaimed. "Yes, that is it exactly. I fear he will trust anyone who appears sympathetic."

"You have offered him sympathy yourself, perhaps?"

"But for no other purpose than to comfort him," Jennifer replied.

"Yet there is someone else?"

"A young lady. Someone I know all too well. She came to Bath prepared to find a husband of the highest rank imaginable."

"An Earl should suit her well enough then."

"That is precisely why I am so much afraid," Jennifer assured him.

"And what comes second on her list?"

"Why, how could you know of her list, sir?"

"I have known many ladies such as that you describe, Miss Damion," he replied grimly. "Wealth is second, I assume. And wealth is there, from all that you have told me. I can see that this is, indeed, a problem."

Jennifer found that his expression frightened her.

"I should not have said as much as I have," she began.

"No. You have been lucid and open, and in return you will receive the best advice that I can give you."

"And what is that, sir?"

"Only that you must determine whether, given the choice, rank or wealth would mean most to her."

Jennifer puzzled for a moment.

"Power is the third ingredient," she said finally. "I have that from her own lips."

"Then, given the changing times, wealth must reign supreme," Sir John replied without a moment's hesitation.

"You are smiling, sir."

"As one in possession of both wealth and power, I have a right to laugh outright if I choose," he said.

"But you are not laughing."

"The matter is too serious for that, if what you say is to be believed."

"But what suggestion have you, sir? You will recall that one was promised."

"I suggest that you tell me when it is and where you are to meet your new friend again. The friend who requires protection."

"Why, tomorrow," Jennifer replied, taken by surprise. "We are to walk on the Crescent. And there I intend to warn him."

"If I have understood you correctly, more than a warning will be in order," he replied. "But do not worry yourself unnecessarily, Miss Damion. I understand the matter better than you think. Meet your friend, by all means. What hour is it that you will be so engaged?"

"At ten."

"Ten it will be then. And now, what think you to a waltz?"

"It is a dance I am not well acquainted with, sir."

"For one as quick as you that should pose no

difficulty," he replied. "Come. Take my arm. And for the moment, if you will, forget your newfound friend and his difficulties. All will be well, I promise you. Do you believe me, Miss Damion?"

Their eyes met for a second time.

"I believe you," Jennifer murmured, taking his arm. "I daresay it does not signify to you one way or the other, but I confess to trusting you quite absolutely."

Chapter Five

It was nearly midnight when Lady Tassing and the two girls arrived back at the house on Gay Street. Agreeing reluctantly that it was no doubt too late for her to "look in" on their uncle, her ladyship made her way to her own rooms while, on entering their own, Susan and Jennifer discovered Jack waiting in the parlor with the news that the Duke had taken advantage of the evening to discover several new symptoms, all of which had given him extraordinary and varied pains, and that it had been necessary to administer a strong dose of laudanum before he could be convinced to retire. As for Molly, the manservant informed them, they would not find her waiting in their chamber since she had declared herself too wearied by certain festivities which had taken place that evening in the servants' hall downstairs to allow her to attend to her mistresses.

"That suits me very well," Susan informed her sister when Jack had taken his leave of them. "Come. Let us shut our bedchamber door so that Uncle will not be disturbed. I have such a great deal to tell you."

And indeed she did not stop talking once while they prepared for bed. It seemed that she had danced every dance with a variety of gentlemen to whom the assiduous Lady Tassing had introduced her, and with some who had presented themselves.

"But that is not the important thing, Jennie," she declared when they were both in bed. "Swear that you will keep a secret if I tell it to you."

Jennifer, whose own concerns had kept her from listening too closely to her sister's chatter, swore with the alacrity of one who wishes to be left in peace and leaned over to snuff the candle.

"I am in love," Susan declared at the same moment darkness descended on them.

"Are you indeed," Jennifer replied wearily.

"But, Jennie, I am quite, quite serious!" Susan cried, giving the bed a bounce. "I did not dance with the gentleman, you understand. In fact I did not meet him until Mr. Cranshaw took me down to supper. And there we happened to sit next to Cousin Amelia, whose companion was quite the most handsome gentleman I ever saw."

"Was he of middle height with mouse-brown hair?" Jennifer demanded, suddenly alert.

"That is not the way I would describe him," Susan said petulantly, "but, yes, I suppose you could say that. Oh, Jennie, he had such a gentle way about him and his eyes—oh, his eyes are soulful. I am certain he has suffered greatly."

"Perhaps his name would serve as a better identification," Jennifer suggested sharply.

"Amelia did not wish to introduce him," Susan replied. "You know what she is. But once I had presented Mr. Cranshaw—such a nice gentleman, but ordinary—one could see at once he has never suffered—she had no choice. Fancy, Jennie. He is an Earl. The first I have ever met, although I declare the title did not matter to me. I wish you had not put out the light, for I would like to see your face when I tell you who he is."

"I fancy you must be speaking of Lord Watching," Jennifer said dryly.

"Oh course I am!" Susan cried. "And you need not pretend you do not know him, for once he heard my name he asked me if I was your sister. You should have seen Amelia's face when he went on to say that he had had some conversation with you earlier and that he found you a most delightful person."

"And what did Cousin Amelia have to say to that?" Jennifer inquired.

"Why, she said that it was too stuffy in the room for her to endure it any longer, and that she thought something was wrong with the salmon. And so, of course, they took their leave, but Jennie—Jennie, you must arrange for me to meet him."

"And do you believe that you can compete with Amelia for his attentions?"

"Oh, surely he is too shy and retiring a sort to interest her for long," Susan replied.

"You will remember that she told us this morning that character did not interest her."

Susan gave a little moan.

"Oh, dear!" she cried. "I had forgotten that."

"She cares a good deal for titles, however," Jennifer went on mercilessly. "One can not do better than an Earl."

"But I must meet him again," Susan sighed. "Oh, Jennie, you have made his acquaintance. Tell me you can manage it. Pray, do not torment me so."

"I meant no torment," Jennifer whispered as her sister turned to nestle like a child in her arms. "The fact is that I am to walk with him tomorrow on the Crescent. And, if you like, you may join us."

Raptures followed, which were thankfully brought to an abrupt halt by Susan falling into a deep sleep, leaving Jennifer to her own thoughts. The outcome of her conversation with Sir John had been a determination to lure Lord Watching's attentions from Amelia, but now a better idea was at hand. Susan should be set to charm him, for her intentions were, at least, sincere. And, besides, the naiveté of both should draw them together. With this hope in mind, she, too, fell asleep, only to awaken to chaos.

Her uncle, it seemed, was dying. At least that was the impression he managed to convey when Jennifer joined him at breakfast. His appetite had left him completely, he assured her, finishing the kippers on his plate with the air of one who must keep up his strength at all cost.

A long recitation of new ailments followed, with frequent references to various medical journals. His heartbeat was irregular, he told her, and his pulse, which he had taken five times since arising, was scarcely that of one who still draws breath. Add to this a liverish complexion, which a hand glass verified to his satisfaction, if not to hers, and sundry evidences that his kidneys were in a state of great disorder.

"Then you must have the doctor called at once," Jennifer declared.

But that, it seemed, was not to be the case.

"That fellow Welsome is a fool!" the Duke declared. "In fact I am convinced that had I not submitted to the baths, I would be my usual self to-day."

"Malingering rather than dying, Uncle?" Jennifer inquired.

"Dying!" Lady Tassing cried.

No one had heard her knock, and, as befitted a close friend, she had let herself in.

"Tell her I cannot have company, gel," the Duke muttered, throwing his handkerchief over his face.

"But of course you must have company!" Lady Tassing declared. "Let me feel your forehead, sir. You know I am quite the expert when it comes to your health. Ah, there seems to be no temperature, but one never knows. One thing is certain. You must not go to the baths this morning. Clearly you are in no state to move from this room. And I will nurse you, sir. Nothing could give me more pleasure, I assure you."

"Of course I will go to the baths!" the Duke roared, suddenly rejuvenated. "Jennifer, see that a sedan chair is called!"

"But, Uncle, only a minute ago you said . . . "

"Never mind what I said, gel! Jack will escort me. It is a pity, Lady Tassing, but I must take my leave of you."

"What a valiant man!" Lady Tassing whispered as he left the room on Jack's arm. "But he should be closely watched. Do you not agree? I think it would be the better part of wisdom if I were to follow. A dip in the waters will do me no harm and I can keep my eye on him."

Hurriedly, she made her departure, no doubt to don an even more attractive dressing gown than the one she was wearing. No sooner had she left the room when Mrs. Capstone entered it, her thin face a mask of misery.

"I'm that sorry to intrude, Miss," she said. "But there's a problem you may be able to help me solve."

"Molly?" Jennifer said wearily. "I have not seen her yet this morning."

"One of my maids who shares her room in the attic attempted to wake her at seven," Mrs. Capstone said, one eye on Jennifer, the other on the floor. "But she said she was too exhausted by last night's celebration, and indeed I think it may be so, for you have never seen such a number of footmen from various houses nearby who saw fit to assemble in the servants' hall while their masters were at the Assembly Rooms. I have always kept an open house, Miss, for I know that servants require their own entertainment. But I assure you, I have never seen anything like the crush . . . Why, they were waiting entry in the street, Miss, and every one claimed a close acquaintance with your abigail."

"It is *too* bad of Molly!" Jennifer exclaimed. "Pray, have her sent to me directly. And if she will not come, I will go to the attic myself and fetch her by hand!"

"Do not be too harsh on her, Jennie!" Susan cried, appearing in the door of the bedchamber as Mrs. Capstone made her retreat. "Besides, there is not time! I do not know how far the Crescent is from here, but it is past nine. What time did you engage to meet Lord Watching?"

"At ten," Jennifer said grimly. And then, looking a second time at her sister, "But why are you wearing my blue taffeta? And what have you done to your hair?"

"I have only frizzed it a bit to be in fashion, Jennie. Oh, do not be out of temper with me!"

"Very well, " Jennifer agreed. "I will be out of temper with Molly instead."

And since, at that moment, their abigail entered the room, rubbing her sleepy eyes, Jennifer was able to be true to her word, with the result that Molly was left with a pile of mending to do which would guarantee her occupation until they returned.

Only when she and Susan were on the street was Jennifer able to turn her attention to the matter at hand. All of which meant that she must give her sister some instruction.

"Lord Watching is only recently come into his title," she said, as they mounted the hill in brilliant sunlight. "He is a retiring gentleman, as you have assumed, and wants nothing more than sympathy. Do you think you can remember that? It may be that he will not be well pleased to see that I have brought you with me, but if you lend an understanding ear . . . "

"Oh, I will listen quite intently, Jennie!"

"You must be yourself," Jennifer warned her. "Chatter, if you like. It will distract him. But do not try to be a lady of the world. It will not suit you."

"I will be anything he likes," Susan assured her. "Oh, Jennie! This must be the Crescent. See how the houses curve about it like a new moon. And is that not Lord Watching there? Yes, it is he. But who is the lady he is talking to? I know it cannot be, but she looks so like . . . "

"Amelia!" Jennifer exclaimed. "Tell me, Susan. Did he mention at supper last night that he was to meet me here?"

"Oh, no! You know, it came as a surprise to me when you said as much. But he could have mentioned it to her before or afterward."

"I can see he must have done," Jennifer said between clenched teeth. "And we are late because of Molly. It's clear he must have assumed that I had broken the appointment. See, she is taking his arm. And now he is handing her into the curricle."

"Call to him!" Susan begged her.

"I will do nothing of the sort," Jennifer replied stiffly. "Amelia has anticipated us, I fear. There is nothing for it but to return to Gay Street."

"I hope that you will reconsider breaking off your walk, Miss Damion," someone said in a low voice.

The color rose in Jennifer's face as she turned to find Sir John Evans standing close beside them.

Chapter Six

Susan was too distraught to do more than acknowledge the introduction to Sir John in an abstracted manner, and while she turned to stare in the direction in which Lord Watching's curricle had disappeared, Jennifer was given an opportunity to speak quietly to her new friend.

"Is this a part of your plan, sir?" she said. "I mean, I recall your asking what time I was to meet the Earl and the spot as well. You are not here by accident, I think."

Sir John nodded. Although there was nothing foppish about his dress, he was outfitted according to fashion in a dark blue coat of superfine, his legs encased in buckskin trousers partly covered by shining Hessian boots. His expression was serious and, altogether, Jennifer found him a reassuring presence.

"I took the liberty of coming here in the hopes that I might meet the gentleman who has aroused your interest and concern, Miss Damion," he said in a low voice. "But unless I am mistaken, I am too late."

"Just as my sister and I were," Jennifer told him. "My uncle delayed us, and then there was the matter of Molly . . . But that does not pertain. The fact is that Lord Watching must have thought I was not coming. I think, perhaps, a certain person was responsible for that."

"The lady you spoke of last evening? The lady with the list?"

"Just so," Jennifer said grimly. "Amelia would stop at nothing. It does not matter on my account, but my sister is greatly disappointed, I fear."

"I think I will return home at once," her sister declared, rousing on hearing herself mentioned. "There is no need for you to accompany me, Jennie. It is only a short distance, and besides I want to be alone."

"Do not sound so doleful, pet," Jennifer reassured her. "There was a misunderstanding over time. Nothing more. And our cousin only happened by . . . "

"You do not believe that and no more do I," Susan declared, starting back around the Crescent at such a great rate that her sister and Sir John had all they could to keep apace with her.

When they reached the house on Gay Street, Susan bobbed a curtsy to Sir John and ran up the stairs without a word, dabbing at her eyes with her fingers.

"I suppose I should go after her," Jennifer said, breathless from the speed of their walk. "You will no doubt wonder why she is in such a state, but it is simply that, like the child she is, she formed an attachment to Lord Watching after seeing him at the ball last night and had set her hopes on meeting him."

"The Earl seems to be an irresistible fellow indeed," Sir John said thoughtfully. "You wish to protect him. A certain lady named Amelia . . . "

"Our cousin, sir."

"All the more complicated. Your cousin wishes to captivate him and your sister hopes simply for a meeting. Ah, well. He is a fortunate gentleman, to be sure. But perhaps there is more to be said on the subject since I can see that for more reason than one it continues to concern you. Could I, perhaps, Miss Damion, convince you to accompany me to the Pump Room? It would be quite proper, I assure you, for, thanks to Lady Tassing, we have been introduced."

"Yes, I believe I would like that well enough," Jennifer agreed. "I believe Susan wishes to be alone, just as she said, and besides, our abigail,

Molly, is at home to keep her company. And I must confess, I would like your advice, sir."

Thus it was that a short time later, they entered the Pump Room arm in arm, to find a great crowd in attendance. Even in the relative dishabille acceptable of a morning, the dandies wore their cravats in all manner of elaborate knots and folds, while ladies of all ages sported vermilion on their cheeks and ribbons in their elaborately coiffured hair. The general uproar was so great that Jennifer and Sir John were forced to find a quiet corner in order to hear one another talk.

"And so it is the Earl of Watching who has aroused your sympathy," Sir John said, his dark eyes hooded.

"You know him then!" Jennifer exclaimed.

"I have never met the gentleman," he assured her, "but I have heard his story, as has everyone else in Bath. He has been fortunate indeed to come into such a great title so unexpectedly."

"I do not think he would agree, sir," Jennifer told him, "for he explained to me that he had had no hopes in that quarter, his uncle who was the former Earl being not many years older than himself."

"That gentleman died in Spain, I believe," Sir John said.

"Yes. Serving under Wellington. An honorable death, if any can be so described. But I am afraid I take a woman's view of such matters."

81

"And what is that, pray?"

"The death of one so young and so full of promise can be nothing but a tragedy, no matter how great the honor," she told him.

"And did you know the former Earl, then?"

"No, I did not, sir, but I have taken his nephew's word on it. He said himself that he could never hope to take his place."

"Sometimes it is not wise to be so humble," Sir John assured her. "He must accept the responsibilities of his position, surely, and not waste his time comparing himself to someone who is now a ghost."

"You take a pragmatic view," Jennifer said with a sigh. "But perhaps you are right. It is not only that he finds himself unworthy, however. Lord Watching told me himself that although, as plain Sir Matthew Fuller, he had his share of friends, he does not know who it is he can call by that name now for the title and the fortune he has inherited make him prey to all sorts, from fond Mamas who wish to marry their daughters to him to . . . "

"He should not have come to Bath then," Sir John said abruptly. "Surely he must have guessed that he would be pandered to. Is there no estate in the country to which he could turn his attention?"

"There is that, sir, but when he went there he was met with nothing but scorn from the agent and others, for it seems that his uncle was a gentleman who knew the science of farming and was

82

making experiments and innovations which Lord Watching does not understand."

"Had he remained in the country he might have come to comprehend them," Sir John suggested. "And yet he came to this spa . . . "

"You are here yourself, sir," Jennifer said sharply, "and so am I, although not at my own bidding. Lord Watching told me that he hoped to find some sort of anonymity here."

"Your friend sounds like a very naive gentleman indeed," Sir John told her. "But no doubt that is why he has excited your sympathy."

"You sound as though you thought he did so deliberately," Jennifer said with rising impatience. "I can assure you that my interest in him would have been of short life, had it not happened that my own cousin is involved. And now my sister."

"I did not say he should not be helped to avoid the charms of the one and recognize those of the other," Sir John protested. "And I am willing, Miss Damion . . . "

"Ah, here you are, Jennifer!" Lady Tassing exclaimed. "And my good Sir! How good to find you two young people in company. Is your mother here this morning, Sir John?"

"I am afraid she is not, my lady," Sir John replied, and Jennifer, remembering that he had told her the evening before that his mother had died fifteen years ago, was surprised to see how easily he dealt with what could have been an embarrassing situation.

"A pity," Lady Tassing said, fluttering her fan in a manner calculated to stir the ringlets of her hair into a perfect flurry. "But, Jennifer, I only came across the room to tell you that your uncle returned from the Baths in a worse temper than I have ever seen him in. It appears, you see, that a certain lady whom he swears he never set eyes on before took certain liberties . . . "

"Perhaps we should speak of this later," Jennifer interrupted her friend, flushing. "Do you think I should return to Gay Street immediately?"

"Oh no, my dear! Do not think of it for a moment, I assure you. I tried my best to explain to him that informality is quite in order in Bath, but he would only groan and place a handkerchief over his face and beg me to leave, although I am certain he did not mean it."

"Then I *should* attend him," Jennifer sighed.

"Only listen to me, my dear, for Molly took a hand in matters at that point and began to recite all manner of scandal to him of the sort that so intrigued your uncle that Jack could not prevail on him to interrupt her in order to take his dose of hartshorn. I cannot think where your abigail gets her information, my dear, for I am liberal-minded enough, as you know, and yet I found it quite impossible to remain in the same room . . . "

"If Uncle cannot be prevailed upon to take his

medicine, then all is well enough," Jennifer said with an air of relief. "I think I always knew that Molly and he would have some point of understanding. No doubt a dose or two of scandal a day will do him far more good than all the hartshorn in the world. But what of Susan, pray? I left her at Gay Street quite distraught, and have been feeling guilty ever after."

"Why, as for your sister, she is well enough," Lady Tassing assured her, "for just before I left the house, the gentleman you danced with last evening appeared to ask after both you and her. It seems he wanted to take you both for a ride in his curricle. Or, perhaps, it was simply you he had arranged to meet on the Crescent. I do not understand the ins and outs of it, but Susan was quite in a glow and agreed to accompany him at once, and she will be in good company because, on leaving the house, I saw your cousin Amelia waiting in the carriage looking very grim. No doubt she hoped to have Sir George Billary to herself and . . . "

"That was the name you introduced me to him as," Jennifer interrupted her. "But, in matter of fact, he is a certain Lord Watching."

"La! I do declare, sometimes I think I am in need of spectacles!" Lady Tassing replied. "But no matter. Your uncle was too intrigued with what Molly was telling him to protest your sister's leaving. And, other than the fact that Lord Watching seemed disappointed that you were not there—

something about a missed appointment, I believe—all has turned out well enough."

With that she darted off, leaving Sir John and Jennifer to stare at one another in amusement.

"And so our Lord Watching has proved himself to be a gentleman," he said in a low voice.

"It was no more than I expected," Jennifer told him. "How furious Amelia must be. But the Earl's regard for the proprieties will not be enough, I assure you, for my cousin is wily in the extreme."

"This news has assured me that the gentleman needs our assistance," Sir John assured her. "Come. Let me tell you my plan."

"Proceed, sir," Jennifer exclaimed, "for no matter what Lady Tassing has said, I believe I must return to my uncle shortly. Molly will amuse him for a time only."

"Then I will be direct," he assured her. "It would seem to me that Lord Watching needs to be taught a simple lesson, to wit that a young gentleman on the town can find many a lady to fall in love with."

"You speak of Susan, sir, or Amelia?"

"The latter should not be encouraged because, it appears, she is unscrupulous. As for your sister, Miss Damion, I do not think she possesses the necessary wiles to teach him the lesson which must be taught. But you . . . "

"You would have me entice him, sir?"

"It is in a good cause, surely. And, as for me,

although I am a simple knight, it might be that I could swerve your cousin from her course."

"But . . .

"The title cannot rival that of an Earl's, I admit," he said with a smile. "But there is money, my dear Miss Damion, and it may be that if I set the rumor abroad . . . "

"To the effect that you are wealthy?"

"Indeed, I have nothing to complain of in that quarter," he assured her. "And of late money has more voice than title. And power follows the former, as I am certain your cousin must realize."

"Then you could have us intrigue to drive Lord Watching and my cousin apart?"

"Are you put off by the suggestion, Miss Damion? It might be that in the process the gentleman would realize the virtues of your sister. Would he not be better off with her than with your cousin?"

"There is no question of that, sir," Jennifer replied.

"Then we are in agreement," he told her, smiling.

"There is only this," Jennifer said. "I do not understand why you should take such an interest in this matter."

His face darkened.

"As it happens," he said in a low voice, "my father once found himself in much the same position as Lord Watching. And he, too, was naive. My stepmother was such a woman as your cousin. And the results were . . . were terrible in the extreme. My father died an unhappy man. I would not want the same for even a stranger such as Lord Watching is to me. Do you understand, Miss Damion? You have your sister's interest at heart. And I have a score to settle against a certain sort of lady. Can we not make an arrangement?"

"I believe we can," Jennifer said thoughtfully. "Very well, sir. Here is my hand."

"And here is mine."

Across the crowded room, Lady Tassing watched the exchange and marveled at it.

Chapter Seven

‗‗

Jennifer returned to the lodging house on Gay Street, fully prepared to find her uncle still being regaled by Molly with the latest scandal, but instead she found their sitting room crowded with a variety of wellborn strangers, all of whom seemed to be talking at once, their remarks addressed, not to one another, but to her uncle, who sat bolt upright in his chair, still clad in his scarlet dressing gown, staring first at one and then the other with a horrified expression, his hand clutched to his heart.

On seeing her come in the door, the Duke of Jennings closed his eyes and slumped sideways in his chair, counterfeiting an attack with such skill that had not Jennifer seen him perform the trick countless times before, she would have been much alarmed. As it was, she took the hint that she was to carry on in his stead, and braced herself to meet the volley of complaints that were leveled at her as her uncle was supported to his bedchamber by the loyal Jack. The cause of the commotion did not long remain a secret, for out of the babel the word "abigail" was repeated often enough for her to realize that Molly had brought all this on their heads.

Jennifer raised one hand to calm the tumult.

"I am Miss Damion, the Duke's niece," she said when all was quiet. "My uncle is not at all well, as you have seen, and it would be best if we could speak quietly and one at a time about whatever seems to be the matter. I gather it concerns Molly."

"If that is the name of your maid, Miss Damion, you are correct indeed," an old gentleman wearing a full wig and a costume which featured bright blue pantaloons announced in an angry voice. "Since your family has arrived in Bath, my footman is nowhere to be found when I want him."

"And mine as well!" an elderly lady whose paisley shawl nearly engulfed her thin face cried. "Such a dedicated fellow as Tom has been after my welfare, no one has ever known, and yet now he is off and out of the house on the slightest pretext. I set my own maid to follow him, and where do you expect he was to be found?"

"Lurking about this house, I warrant!" another lady explained. "Along with my Will."

"And my Frank!"

"And my Bob!"

Seeing that they were off again in concert with one another, Jennifer raised her hand again, pretending a certain calm which she was very far indeed from feeling.

"I must apologize for my abigail's charms, I see," she said evenly. "I fear that my response to you would be that you are in charge of your own servants, and if you cannot keep them in control, so much the worse. But I know that my uncle would reply otherwise, were he able, and I am all but certain that he will relieve your minds by sending Molly back to the country immediately."

A general sigh of relief swept like a strong wind through the room. At the same moment Molly poked her head around the door leading to Jennifer's and Susan's bedchamber and cried, "Oh no, Miss! I will change my ways, I swear it!"

"Indeed you will not!" the Duke declared, and the company's heads turned as one to the other side of the sitting room where the Duke of Jennings, supported by Jack, stood in the doorway of his own chamber.

"Keep your own households in order any way you see best, my friends!" he cried with a vigor unlikely in one who only minutes before had been, to all appearances, at death's door. "The fact of the matter is that my nieces cannot spare their abigail and that is all I have to say on the subject. Good morning, ladies! Good morning, gentlemen!"

Startled, they began to file out of the sitting room and Jennifer saw Mrs. Capstone, who had evidently been listening to the commotion from the landing, hurrying down the stairs before them.

As soon as the last was gone, the Duke came into the room, miraculously recovered from the need of Jack's assistance.

"And now, you jade!" he said to Molly. "Come and finish your story about the Duchess of Wanestead and her groom. I declare you were wasted in the country!"

Not knowing whether to be angry at the ordeal her uncle had put her to or amused at his sudden turnabout regarding Molly, Jennifer went into the room she shared with Susan and found her sister curled on the bed, stifling a fit of giggles with her handkerchief.

"Oh, what a lovely day it has been, Jennie!" she cried. "What a sketch Uncle is! Do you not agree? And Molly is so clever. She must have guessed that something like this would happen and you should have seen the way she set to wooing Uncle. They were gossiping when I went off on my ride with Lord Watching and Amelia, and they were

92

still at it, hammer and tongs, when I returned. And see how he comes back for more! I declare I have not heard him ask for his medicine once since Molly began her stories. Do you suppose she is making them up especially to charm him?"

"Considering the number of friends she has made these few days, I expect she speaks more of the truth than one would like to suppose," Jennifer replied dryly. "What a rascal she is! And, as Uncle said, she was wasted in the country, for he has little interest in the affairs of the servants' hall, and that was all the news she had at her disposal when we were isolated there. But now she is better than the *Gazette*! Quite indispensable!"

"Enough of Molly!" Susan cried, springing from the bed and embracing her sister. "Oh, I have had a lovely morning. Imagine, Lord Watching himself . . . "

"Lady Tassing told me," Jennifer assured her, allowing Susan to waltz her about the room. "It was good of him to come here, for he had reason enough to suppose that I had not cared to make my appointment with him."

"Oh, he was so full of regrets that he should have missed you," Susan assured her. "What a perfect gentleman he is, Jennie, and so handsome. I declare I could not keep my eyes away from him! And Amelia was so annoyed. You would have laughed to see the way she tossed her head when he handed me into the curricle. I'm sure she had

93

meant to keep him to herself. You know, of course, that she schemed the meeting. She heard him mention it last night over supper, I suppose. And what a position she was put in, for when she met him on the Crescent, supposedly quite by chance, she told him that she understood that you were to be kept at home by Uncle's health. What a delight it was to me to be able to call her hand."

"What did you say, then?" Jennifer demanded.

"Why, nothing but the truth. That you had gone to meet him and had been kind enough to allow me to accompany you. But that we had been delayed and had arrived at the appointed spot just in time to see him and Amelia driving away. Lord Watching said that if Amelia had not told him what she had of Uncle, he would have waited. Oh, he was all apologies! And then Amelia was forced to say that she must have been mistaken. And then we rode out of town into the country and . . . "

"Did he seem much charmed by our cousin?" Jennifer interrupted.

Susan's face fell into a pout.

"I declare I think he was," she said, "although I expected that he would see through her deceit concerning you. But Lord Watching is very . . ."

"Naive?"

"I would prefer to call him good-natured," Susan told her. "Oh, dear, what a dreadful thing it would be if he allowed her to charm him!"

"What was his attitude toward you?" Jennifer

94

asked, pretending to examine herself in the pier glass.

"Why, to be honest, I think he sees me as little more than a child," Susan said sadly. "At first he would only ask after you, but when I assured him that you had gone to the Pump Room with a certain gentleman of your acquaintance . . . "

"You did not name names?"

"Indeed I did not, because I could not remember it. Besides, it was clear that Amelia was curious, and even had I known I would not have given her the satisfaction."

"And how did Lord Watching take the information?" Jennifer asked her.

"Why, he was disappointed clear enough, but he declared he was glad your morning had not been ruined and then Amelia went on to hint that you were the sort of young lady who had many strings to her bow."

"Did she indeed!" Jennifer exclaimed. "I think our cousin will make me a worthy opponent!"

"What do you mean by that?" Susan demanded. "What makes you so grim, Jennie?"

"It is nothing," her sister assured her. For a moment only she was tempted to disclose the arrangement she and Sir John had made, and then she bethought herself that were she to confide in Susan that she meant to trifle with Lord Watching's heart she would be setting a poor example. Let it be enough for the time to set herself to wooing him away from Amelia. If Susan was troubled by the turn events might take, all could be explained.

"Come," she said. "Let us discuss what we will wear to the Assembly this evening. I think for you the yellow satin and as for me . . . "

By evening both girls were arrayed as elegantly as their wardrobes would allow and it was with some amusement that they passed through the sitting room to find a weary Molly still being plied with questions by their indefatigable uncle.

"She has been hoist on her own petard, I think," Jennifer whispered as they went out the door to join Lady Tassing on the landing.

It had been arranged that they should travel to the Assembly Room with Lady Daphne and Amelia and the carriage was awaiting them. As soon as they were settled comfortably together, Lady Tassing began to talk in some state of excitement.

"How clever of you, Jennifer," she said, "to have made such a friend of Sir John Evans!"

"Evans," Amelia said in a languid voice. "I do not believe I know the name."

"But you should, my dear," Lady Tassing assured her. "Your mother told me of your list, and his name should go on it at once, for even though he is a mere knight, it seems he has inherited a great fortune."

It was not yet dusk and Jennifer saw her cousin sit to attention.

"I wish you would not be so free with your talk about my list, Mama," she said in an irritated voice. "But since you know of it, Lady Tassing, pray go on. Who is this fellow?"

"I knew his mother well," Lady Tassing assured her, much to Jennifer's suppressed amusement. "Poor woman. When he returned from escorting you home, Jennie, he made a point of telling me that she was dead and had been these fifteen years. I could only tell him that time flies, I was that embarrassed! But the point is that his father is dead, as well, and he is in possession of a considerable fortune. He did not tell me this outright, you understand, for he is not the sort to vaunt himself, but I would ask questions. Having known his mother so well, that was only natural, surely."

"Surely," Jennifer echoed, thinking how clever Sir John had been to spread the news in such a certain fashion.

"Seeing how interested he was in you, my dear, I thought that I should make myself knowledge-able," Lady Tassing told her. "And he was properly modest, of course, as a gentleman should be. But I discovered that he is in possession of three large estates, not to mention property in London, and there is a good deal besides, I believe."

"Three estates!" Amelia exclaimed. "And only a knight?"

"Times have changed since I was a gel," Lady Tassing assured her. "Money is drifting downward. Sir John's father was a great businessman, I believe. And from what the gentleman said, I believe he inherits a flair for investment. Great titles are all very well, but money is what matters nowadays."

"Have you made a mental note of that, Amelia?" Lady Daphne said dryly as their carriage swayed over the cobblestones.

"What does all this mean, Jennie?" Susan whispered.

"It may well mean that our cousin will lose her interest in Lord Watching," Jennifer replied in an undertone. "Say nothing!"

And so they all remained silent as Lady Tassing praised Sir John Evans to the skies and it was with a thoughtful expression that Amelia allowed the coachman to help her from the carriage.

Lord Watching was waiting just inside the door to the Assembly Room. His eyes lit up when he saw Jennifer, but Amelia did not appear to notice.

"Is Sir John Evans here?" Jennifer heard her murmur to Lady Tassing.

"My dear, that is the gentleman making his way toward us! I expect he will ask Jennifer to join him in the cotillion."

"Lord Watching has claimed the first dance," Jennifer told her, trying not to see the hurt in Susan's eyes.

"Then I would like to be introduced to Sir John

Evans," Amelia was heard to say in a determined tone.

And as Jennifer drifted away on Lord Watching's arm, she saw the two meet. For a moment Sir John turned from Amelia and met Jennifer's eyes. A smile passed between them. Moments later, as the orchestra struck up a tune, Jennifer saw him enter the line with Amelia, who was smiling in a particularly self-satisfied manner, and knew that the game had begun in earnest.

Chapter Eight

The week which followed was filled with a perfect whirl of activities, only some of which were dictated by the routine of Bath society. With Lady Tassing and Susan as chaperones, the two couples not only attended routs and balls and soirées, but made up their own entertainment as well. Rides were taken into the hilly country to the north of the city and picnics were enjoyed in sunny spots. One day they traveled in the opposite direction as far as Bristol and savored the excitement of that thriving port.

Fortunately the Duke's health was as excellent as he would allow it to be, thanks to the ministrations of the faithful Jack and Molly's stories, which, like Scheherazade's, seemed to be endless, although Jennifer was amused to hear that pretty miss plead with her master to allow her more time to herself, reminding him that unless she kept up her former connections and made others beside, she would not be in possession of the latest gossip. The Duke remarked on the reasonableness of this suggestion, but thought it best that she collect her news in the morning while he was at the baths, whereupon an unseemly wrangle ensued in which Molly insisted that the best time to hear scandal was at night when her friends had the opportunity to sit together and exchange the news of the day in the servants' quarters, and the Duke protested that evening was just the time when he himself liked to be so regaled. Somehow a compromise was reached, but it was apparent to Jennifer that Molly was kept so busy asking questions that she had little time for her usual amusements. At all events, there were no more complaints from their neighbors that their footmen were being distracted from their work.

Such relative peace would not last, of course. Jennifer knew Molly too well to fancy that she could long be kept from rebellion. And it was the same, she thought, when it came to the frivolity which she and the others were enjoying, since it was in essence a charade.

Not that she and Sir John had continued to scheme together. There was no time for that since they were never alone together. But their plan had been blessed by its simplicity. At first Lord Watching had been bewildered by Amelia's shift of attention to Sir John, but he gave no sign of being unduly disturbed, appearing to enjoy Jennifer's company quite thoroughly. As for Amelia, she glowed with satisfaction at her apparent coup, puffing and preening herself every moment she was in Sir John's presence and taking great pride in his seeming enjoyment of a conversation which she littered with feeble attempts at wit and a variety of miscellaneous facts, most of which dealt with the history of Bath, a subject which she had obviously studied at some length for reasons known only to herself.

"Even though she *is* my daughter, I cannot think what attracts Sir John to her," Lady Daphne said one afternoon when, having replaced Lady Tassing as chaperone on an outing, she and Jennifer found themselves alone for a few minutes. "Sir John seems such an intelligent gentleman. Indeed I often think I see an ironic expression in his eyes when he is making such a show of listening to her ramble on. And yet he persists in making himself her companion."

Had her aunt been the sort to place a high value on her daughter at the marriage mart, Jennifer would have felt guilty. As it was, she was tempted to tell Lady Daphne the truth. And yet she resisted, murmuring something about gentlemen's tastes. It was not, she assured herself, as though any harm was being done, for Amelia gave no sign of falling hopelessly in love. Indeed, Jennifer did not believe her cousin capable of passion. She was far too pragmatic for that particular emotion and it was obvious that if she made any metaphor of her new admirer it was that of a prize she had won with her own inimitable charm.

As for Sir John, he played his role remarkably well. Assiduous in his attentions as he was, he would draw back almost inperceptibly whenever Amelia behaved in too confident a manner. From the beginning he made it clear that he was to be at no one's beck and call, and whenever Amelia overreached herself, he was able, by subtle means, to remind her that, for the present, they remained no more than friends.

"How I wish that I could have his confidence," Lord Watching told Jennifer one day when they were picnicking beside a stream which glittered in the summer sunlight. "I swear, I admire him unduly, and intend to make him my model."

"I think you are mistaken in that," Susan said in a rush, having managed, as always, to stay close to him.

"What makes you say that?" Lord Watching asked her curiously. "Dash it if he is not the sort of gentleman any fellow like myself might hope to be."

"Why, as to that," Susan said, flushing, "I only mean that I always feel that there is something hidden about him. Sometimes I think that he is laughing at my cousin. Not that she does not deserve it. But . . . Oh, dear, I should not have said that, I expect. Indeed, I should not be here at all!"

And rising, she hurried away from them, all golden curls and ribbons.

"I believe I have upset the child," Lord Watching exclaimed, starting to his feet.

"First of all," Jennifer said calmly, "my sister is no child. You would do well to realize that and treat her accordingly, sir. And secondly, I think I know what she meant to say, which is that you do very well as yourself."

"Do you really mean that, Miss Damion?" he said, staring down at her. "I know I lack self-confidence, but . . . "

"You should try to think of yourself as the thoughtful, sensitive person you really are," Jennifer assured him. "I declare I have never known anyone as honest and open as you are, sir, and I believe you make too bad a habit of underrating yourself, if you take my meaning."

"Perhaps you are right," Lord Watching said in a low voice, "and yet when I consider Sir John . . . "

He turned to look at that gentleman, who, seated beside Amelia some distance away, was nibbling some grapes and listening in a distracted manner to that young lady's chatter. And yet, in the next moment, something she said seemed to truly amuse him, and he broke into delighted laughter which brought roses to Amelia's lovely cheeks.

For a moment Jennifer was aware of a sensation of falling. It was as though the world had somehow lost its hold on her and she realized that, although all of this might have begun as a game, both she and Sir John might have underestimated the power of her cousin's beauty. And yet, she told herself in the next instance, what did it matter if he should find himself truly attracted to Amelia? Were he to make an alliance with her cousin, he would do it with open eyes. And the original purpose of all this would have been served. Lord Watching had been saved.

That evening she found that she welcomed the distraction provided by her uncle's affairs. Molly, showing the first signs of rebellion since he had threatened to remove her from Bath, did not return at the appointed hour, and the Duke, after first railing against the girl in no uncertain fashion, found it convenient to imagine that he was being attacked by a fit of gout.

When various doses of medicine seemed to bring him no relief and even the patient Jack was at his wit's end, Jennifer determined on a last resort and, leaving Susan to his mercy, hurried up the stairs to Lady Tassing's rooms.

"Why, of course I will come at once, my dear!" her ladyship exclaimed, beaming broadly. "I declare I have neglected your uncle of late, what with all our expeditions. What a pleasure it will be to me to bring him the comfort of my presence. No one has ever realized as well as I how much the poor man suffers!"

Returning with her friend in tow, Jennifer was rewarded by seeing her uncle sit up straighter in his chair, a look of trepidation on his thin face.

"Now, I have come to comfort you, sir," Lady Tassing declared, drawing a chair close to his, apparently forgetful of the fact that she had neglected to remove her nightcap and that her face, without favor of vermilion or powder, wore an unfamiliar aspect. "Tell me about the pain in detail, do! You know how that comforts you."

"Why, Damme, I believe the attack has passed!" the Duke of Jennings exclaimed.

Lady Tassing made no secret of her disappointment.

"Well then, sir, you can recollect it," she announced. "What purpose is there in suffering if you cannot share it with your friends? And I am a great friend, am I not?"

The Duke protested weariness, but it was no good. In all conscience he could not walk unaided to his bedchamber after the fuss he had just created, and Jennifer saw to it that Jack was dismissed with a flicker of her eyes. It was with some considerable amusement that she sat the next half hour and listened to her uncle prevaricate the most alarming symptoms, to all of which Lady Tassing listened with great attention, from time to time passing one hand over the Duke's brow, which was, she declared, feverish.

But such diversions could not last long. Molly returned and, after being berated in a fashion which one would not have thought such an ailing gentleman capable of, promised never to be so late again. Lady Tassing took her leave with reluctance, promising to stop in the next morning before the Duke left for the baths in order to be acquainted with the manner in which he had spent the night before she accompanied Susan and Jennifer on an outing which had been planned for that afternoon.

And so it was that the next day, under a sultry sun, Jennifer found herself alone with Lord Watching, who had proposed a stroll along the country lane which bordered the meadow which the company had chosen for their picnic. Aware that Susan's eyes were fastened on them wistfully, Jennifer had agreed reluctantly, and in a few minutes she and Lord Watching were walking arm in arm in the shelter of a hawthorn hedge.

Lord Watching seemed ill at ease, commenting inappropriately on the flora and fauna, all of which he called by the wrong names, identifying honeysuckle as roses and a rook as a pheasant. It was clear that he was nervous and Jennifer was soon to learn the reason why.

"You cannot imagine, my dear Miss Damion," he said finally after a great clearing of the throat, "how much these past few weeks have meant to me."

"We have entertained ourselves most enjoyably indeed," Jennifer replied, removing her arm from his. "And now, I think, we should turn about and rejoin the others."

"But first I must say what—what I have determined to say!" Lord Watching exclaimed. "That is, if I can remember the words. I had them by heart last night, I assure you, and yet now . . . "

Jennifer turned away from him. She had not wanted to be cruel, but now, guessing what he was about to hint at, she realized that she had done more than teach him that Amelia was not the only young lady whom he might find attractive. She had in all truth not supposed that he would fancy himself in love with her. Or was that only a deceit? Had she not somehow entertained the thought . . .

But no! Her attention had been focused on Amelia. Amelia, who could not be hurt. But Lord Watching was vulnerable. How careless she had been not to recognize the fact that, having given him so much of her company, it might come to this.

And yet she must not allow him to speak the words. No more must she encourage him to seek an interview with her uncle. And yet, where was the way out? For a moment she found herself thinking with resentment of Sir John. He, at least, was clever enough to have anticipated this moment. How was it he had not warned her, unless . . .

"It is better to say nothing," she said in an even voice, "unless the words come naturally. Now, tell me, what do you fancy this flower is? I have never seen such yellow bugles. Do you suppose it is some sort of lily?"

She had disconcerted him, just as she had intended, and as he went to examine the flower she had indicated, Jennifer felt quite thoroughly ashamed of herself. The question might have been avoided for today, but how was she to continue to circumvent it? Only by refusing to be his partner on further expeditions, no doubt. And yet he would be hurt were she to brush him aside as Amelia had done.

When they rejoined the others, she saw that Sir John was watching her anxiously. He was clever enough, of course, to have guessed what might have happened. As the picnic things were packed away in the curricles, Jennifer made an effort to speak to him alone, but Amelia was constantly at his elbow, rattling on about this and that. Thus it was that Jennifer found herself returning to Bath in a carriage with Susan and Lord Watching, both of whose eyes never seemed to leave her face. For the first time in her life, Jennifer pleaded a migraine and, as soon as they reached Gay Street, retreated to her chamber to consider the damage she might have done.

Chapter Nine

The next morning Jennifer rose, determined on two courses of action. In the first place, she would explain to Susan precisely why she had made herself so agreeable to Lord Watching and that, despite appearances, she thought of that gentleman only as a friend. Secondly, she would send some excuse to release her from the engagement she had made for another outing that afternoon, for although she could not think she had been wrong in demonstrating to Lord Watching that he could find many young ladies attractive, it was clearly cruel to encourage him now that his affections had been aroused.

Her first plan was thwarted, however, when Susan, looking pale and listless, announced soon after breakfast that she intended to spend the morning on a shopping expedition with Lady Tassing. Indeed, she made it so clear to Jennifer through various devices that she did not wish to have any sort of intimate conversation that to have persisted would have been folly.

Her uncle, having gone to the baths with Jack in attendance, and Molly, inexplicably, nowhere in sight, Jennifer proceeded to write a note to Amelia, excusing herself from the entertainment planned for the afternoon. But no sooner had she seated herself at the escritoire than a knock sounded at the sitting-room door and Mrs. Capstone, sharp-nosed as usual, announced Lady Daphne and Amelia herself.

For the first time Jennifer received more than a peck on the cheek from her cousin. Lady Daphne, on the contrary, seemed singularly subdued.

"You cannot think what has happened, Jennie!" Amelia exclaimed, tossing her head like a thoroughbred prepared to run a race.

"Perhaps we should say what *may* happen, my dear," her mother suggested.

"I have not the slightest doubt that it *will* happen," Amelia reproved her. "Do you think I would have come here with the news had I not been quite certain?"

"I do not think you can be *quite* certain," Lady Daphne replied.

"I am not one to make mistakes, Mother!" Amelia cried petulantly. "Come! Only tell me of a mistake I have made recently. One mistake! Surely that is not too much to ask."

"I do not share your penchant for keeping records," Lady Daphne retorted. "All the same, I think that, at the very least, you are being premature."

"Premature!" Amelia cried. "When have you ever known me to be premature, pray. Be specific, do, if you are to make accusations!"

"You are impossible to argue with, my dear," her mother said flatly, taking a seat and proceeding to fan herself rapidly, although the day was rather cool.

"Now, in that you are quite correct," Amelia said, pacified. "Perhaps you will allow me to share my great news with my cousin now."

"I do not know how you can share news that is no news," Lady Daphne insisted, "for news is based on fact, I believe. However, say what you like. There is no way of stopping you. And besides, Jennifer must find this argument tedious."

As it happened, Jennifer had found it anything but tedious, since she had been overcome, in the process of their wrangling, by a great sense of foreboding.

"Well, Cousin, my news is to this point," Amelia declared, whirling about in a great display of exhilaration. "Sir John Evans means to announce for me!"

Jennifer's first thought was that surely he had not allowed the game he played to go that far. And her second was that perhaps she had been mistaken about the attitude he had taken toward Amelia. Perhaps when she had thought he was laughing at her cousin he had, indeed, been laughing with her. And yet surely Sir John knew Amelia for what she was. It had been he, after all, who had spread the news that he was a wealthy man for the express purpose of luring Amelia away from Lord Watching. As a consequence, he must know that any interest she showed him was firmly grounded in mercenary motives.

"Are you quite certain?" Jennifer said in a low voice.

"La, now you sound like Mother," Amelia fretted. "What is there so difficult to believe about it, I ask you? You have seen for yourself how attentive Sir John has been to me of late. Not a day has passed but that we have been together and you have been witness to the degree of attention he has paid me."

"Is that the basis for your belief that he will offer?" Jennifer demanded. "For if it is . . . "

"Do not play Job's comforter with me!" Amelia exclaimed. "I have heard quite enough of that sort of thing from Mama already. Of course I have better reason to think that he may offer! Certain remarks he made only yesterday were quite enough in themselves. A gentleman does not speak of certain matters lightly. But those are personal matters. Quite, quite private, I assure you and I do not care to repeat a word that has passed between us. The important thing is that I am certain of the outcome, as I have said before."

Jennifer, who at first had been quite prepared to hear nothing more from her cousin than the usual self-deluding comments, found herself forced to think again. Granted that she knew Sir John's original intent well enough. But as Amelia had said, there were certain things that gentlemen did not say unless they were serious in their intentions. And since she could not believe that her friend had gone so far as to play the cad, she suddenly faced the fact that her cousin might, indeed, be speaking truly enough. As to why that possibility should make her feel as she did, Jennifer was not certain, unless it was that she could not bear the thought that Sir John had allowed himself to be caught in the web of Amelia's charming ways.

Luckily Amelia was too full of herself to notice that Jennifer greeted the subsequent congratulatory remarks she proceeded to make with less than enthusiasm. As they left, however, with Amelia all in a flutter to meet Sir John at the Pump Room, Jennifer thought she noticed her aunt looking at her in a speculative way.

There was no time to concern herself with what Lady Daphne might or might not have guessed, however, for no sooner had her guests' carriage clattered up Gay Street when the Duke of Jennings returned from the baths with the faithful Jack in attendance.

"I want a word with you, Miss!" her uncle declared, waving a letter in front of Jennifer's face. "Mrs. Capstone handed it me as I came up the stairs and, having opened it forthwith—for you know I never make a delay with correspondence no matter what the state of my health—I discover that a certain Earl of Watching seeks an interview with me."

Jennifer felt herself grow pale.

"And why should you think that concerns me, Uncle?" she said in a low voice. "Indeed I hope that it does not."

"I am not a dunderhead, Miss!" the Duke exclaimed, lowering himself heavily into his chair. "Watching is the fellow you and your sister have been on countless outings with, I believe. Eh? Eh?"

"That is so, Uncle," Jennifer admitted, her mind racing.

"Well, then, it follows that either you or young Susan have caught yourself a prize, does it not? For I can only think of one reason that a young gentleman who is, after all, a total stranger to me should ask for an interview. My salts, Jack. There's a good fellow! I declare, good news as well as bad brings on these damnable palpitations. I am not a well man yet. Indeed I think I never will be for this morning . . . "

"Uncle!" Jennifer cried, throwing herself down on the footstool at his feet. "Listen to me, do. It has all been a great misunderstanding. I tried to hint as much to Lord Watching only yesterday and, indeed, I have promised myself never to see him again in private company."

"Then it is you he wishes to speak to me about, eh?" the Duke declared, gulping his medicine and assuming a sour expression. "Watching intends to declare for you, eh, and you are intent on making some mischief about what should be a simple enough matter."

"There is nothing at all simple about it," Jennifer assured him, "for I do not wish to entertain any proposal from that direction!"

"Is he a scoundrel then, Miss?"

"Why, he is anything but! I declare I have never met a better-natured person."

"Then he is bankrupt and seeks to make a fortune on you."

"Oh no, Uncle! He possesses a considerable fortune and he is no spendthrift."

"Well then," the Duke declared in a puzzled manner, "I can make no sense out of your attitude, gel. This fellow's title outweighs mine—which is no small matter in itself. Neither his fortune nor his character are in question. He wishes to speak

117

with me. And you ramble on about misunderstandings."

"It is only that I am extremely fond of him," Jennifer told him, "and, as a consequence, he must not be allowed to speak for me."

"Ah, we are to deal with paradoxes, are we?" the Duke replied. "The hartshorn, Jack! I feel a strange sensation in my stomach. But puzzles have ever affected me, thus, I should think you would take more regard for me, Miss."

"It is because I am fond of Lord Watching that I do not wish to disappoint him," Jennifer explained with a rising note of urgency in her voice as she saw how determined her uncle was not to understand.

"If you are *fond* there need be no disappointment, gel," the Duke replied. "You had always been *fond* of logic, I believe. Fault me in that!"

"I think of him as a brother, sir," Jennifer replied.

"Excellent, Miss! Excellent! I only wish that such kindly feelings had existed between your late aunt and myself. And yet, despite all this, you wish me not to see him."

"I do not love him, Uncle!" Jennifer cried in despair.

"Well, as for love," the Duke of Jennings said disparagingly, "I think you set your sights too high."

"This is intolerable, sir!" Jennifer announced,

118

rising with a certain dignity. "Since you persist in misunderstanding me, let me put it to you thus. The Earl of Watching mistook friendship for something more. I do not wish to be put in a position to refuse him point-blank. If I can only be given a few days in which to demonstrate that I will gladly remain his friend but that nothing more can be hoped for . . . "

"You mean to say that if I grant the fellow an interview and declare that I am agreeable enough to his making a proposal, you will refuse him?"

"Indeed I must, Uncle. Do not put me in that position, pray. You can always make the excuse of your health. Only a few days' grace will be enough for me to prevent him from making an open declaration to you."

"I declare, I do not understand you, gel," the Duke told her. "New times! New ways! My gout is paining me again. Yes, Jack. Raise my leg just so. Damme, I can remember a time when no one would have refused an Earl. I take it as a personal insult, gel. Earls have their privileges!"

"Well, as for that, I am not one of them!" Jennifer exclaimed, angry now. "Make an excuse of your health, I beg you, Uncle!"

"Well, as for that, until this discussion with you, Miss, I have never felt better, and I think I must speak for myself. If Watching wishes to speak to me I can do no better than to assure him that I feel he is a worthy candidate for your hand. Bring

119

me paper and a quill, Jack. And turn your face away if you can put no better expression on it, Miss. Now, where is Molly?"

As though on cue a knock sounded on the door and Mrs. Capstone made her entrance in an obvious state of extreme distress.

"Oh, Your Grace!" she cried. "I do not know how to put it to you, but I have just received word that your daughters' abigail has eloped with Lord Bemis's footman!"

His reply to Lord Watching instantly forgotten, the Duke gave way first to a torrent of wrath and then to an onslaught of pain which assaulted every member of his body with the result that Jack and Jennifer and even Mrs. Capstone were sent scurrying about the room in search of various remedies, all of which, despite his agony, the Duke demanded in a specific manner. Relief finally came in the form of Lady Tassing who, having returned from her shopping expedition with Susan, seemed quite overjoyed at the sight of the patient in extremity. Her first move was to pass her cool hands up and down the Duke's face with the result that he demanded to be taken to his bedroom and that the doctor—quack though he undoubtedly was—be called at once.

"Only do not ministrate to me in person, Lady Tassing!" he pleaded as Jack supported him from the room.

But before he had gained his chamber, a knock

sounded on the door, and Jennifer, going to open it, was dismayed to find Sir John Evans standing on the landing.

"What is the matter?" he demanded as Mrs. Capstone darted past him on her way to send a message to the doctor. "There seems to be a certain confusion . . . "

"Damme, is this Watching?" the Duke of Jennings demanded. "I am too sick to see you, sir! And yet, on second thought, perhaps it would be as well if we could be alone together. The ladies gone, you understand! All ladies gone!"

He spoke with such emphasis as to cause Susan and Lady Tassing to flee the room, but Jennifer kept her stand.

"I will not have you make a comedy of errors out of this, Uncle," she said in a determined voice. "This is not Lord Watching, but rather Sir John Evans, who is a friend you must have heard me speak of."

"And do you intend to declare for this jade too, sir?" the Duke demanded, letting Jack lead him back to his chair. "She has been busier than I would have thought possible, I see."

"No, he does not wish to declare anything, Uncle!" Jennifer exclaimed in despair.

A glance at Sir John assured her that he understood something of the situation she found herself in.

"I am sorry to find you in ill health, Lord Jennings," he said in a low voice. "Perhaps my visit is inopportune. But before I leave, I might mention that my second cousin was a great victim of the gout and he discovered a marvelous remedy which perhaps I might share with you."

The Duke was all attention immediately. Requesting that his visitor take a seat, he at once began to indulge himself in a recitation of the various illnesses which had afflicted him over the years, and for each one Sir John offered a suggestion, it appearing that every member of his family, indeed every friend and acquaintance, had at some time been cured of every imaginable affliction. Jennifer, who had taken a seat in the corner of the room, listened incredulously as her uncle became more and more confidential, coming at last to the business of Molly.

"That need be no more than a tiresome distraction, sir, if you will allow me to say it," Sir John declared. "For if what you tell me of her character is a true reflection of it, she will be back with you in no time at all. I know Lord Bemis well, and I do not think he will let any footman of his go so easily."

Within the half hour the Duke of Jennings seemed completely reassured. The pain in his foot had lessened, he declared, and as for his stomach, he believed that after he had rested for an hour he could endure the sight of oyster patties. Jack, having escorted him to his chamber, went off in search of Mrs. Capstone with the order and Jennifer found herself alone with Sir John.

For a moment there was silence between them. His eyes were hooded and she could not guess what he was thinking.

"I came because of what I believe happened between you and Lord Watching yesterday," he said finally in a low voice. "He intends to declare himself for you, does he not?"

"I tried to dissuade him," Jennifer began. "But he is such an innocent that no doubt he took my disclaimers for delicacy. I fault myself, sir, for though our scheme seemed an excellent one at the time, I did not imagine that I would be forced to hurt him because of it. That is the danger of games, sir, and, although you may have found yours satisfying enough . . ."

"I do not understand your reference," Sir John said coldly. "What concerns me is character, Miss Damion, and I see that Lord Watching has demonstrated little enough of that, since at one moment he fancies himself in love with your cousin and now, apparently, with you."

"The fault, if there is any, does not lie with him, sir!" Jennifer exclaimed. "His heart is easily led, I grant you, but that is not a fault."

"What call you it otherwise?" he demanded.

"A weakness, perhaps. No more. No less. We are all granted certain weaknesses, surely."

"I am not certain I agree," Sir John said grimly.

123

"You are too eager to be the judge!" Jennifer declared angrily. "What should it matter to you whether Lord Watching is weak or strong? He is a gentleman, either way. Which is more than I can claim in your name, sir!"

"I will not ask you to explain yourself," he said, rising. "Although I must confess that I thought better of you than that you would express yourself in riddles."

"There is no riddle," Jennifer told him. "I only say to you that I will play games no longer."

"And I agree," he told her. "It is obvious to me that, no matter how you think you feel, Lord Watching's future is of more concern to me than any other. So be it! If you fault me for the scheme we planned, so be that, too! Good morning, Miss Damion. And I must thank you, although for what, it is not the time for you to know."

Chapter Ten

The angry interview had the effect of making Jennifer determined to end all pretense of charade, on her part at least. She would, she told herself, explain everything to Susan at the first opportunity. More than that, rather than avoiding Lord Watching, which would be, she saw now, to take the coward's course, she would simply try to make him see that he had mistaken infatuation for love and urge him not to allow his heart to lead him willy-nilly wherever a young lady showed an interest in him. She would take care to remind him that only a few short weeks ago, Amelia had engaged his affection and that . . .

Her reflections were interrupted by her sister's return from Lady Tassing's rooms. Susan seemed in a strange, restless state and listened in a distracted manner to Jennifer's explanation of how she had excused herself from their engagement with Lord Watching and the others for that afternoon.

"You, of course, are free to go," she went on, "for I believe it has been arranged that our aunt has agreed to act as chaperone."

She had thought that Susan's response would be one of pleasure since she was to be so unexpectedly given the opportunity to be Lord Watching's companion, but instead her sister continued to pace the room, apparently lost in thought.

"I wonder if Uncle would advance me next quarter's allowance," she said suddenly, pausing before the mirror over the mantelpiece to fidget with her blond curls with uncustomary nervousness.

"Why, you know how he is about such things," Jennifer replied, puzzled. "Are you in need of new gowns? For if you are I can spare you a few guineas. Only let the dressmaker send the bill to me instead of you and spare the lecture Uncle will give you for being spendthrift."

Susan turned to her with a sly look, so much unlike her usual expression that Jennifer was startled.

"That would be good of you, Jennie," she said. "But would it not be just as simple if you would lend me the guineas now? Outright, that is?"

"But you know full well the woman will not expect to be paid in advance," Jennifer argued. "That is not the way of things."

"I declare, you may as well forget I asked you then," Susan said fretfully. "Indeed, I did not ask you. I think it unpleasant of you, Jennie, to make an offer you do not mean."

"And I think that you should tell me what this is all about," Jennifer said in a low voice. "I know you too well, Sister, to think that you would act so strangely all because of a new gown or two. Besides, it is a matter that may be settled at any time. As it is, the hour approaches one and you must want to prepare yourself for this afternoon's expedition."

"I—I believe that I will send my regrets as well," Susan told her, going to the escritoire and taking up a quill pen which she then proceeded to look at with the expression of someone who has never seen such an object before.

"But why should you do any such thing?" Jennifer demanded. "Something has happened, Susan, and you must tell me what it is."

"La, but you always treat me like a child," her sister said in a low voice which quavered strangely.

"I only mean to help you if something is troubling you," Jennifer said gently.

For a moment her sister hesitated and then, dropping the pen, she ran to embrace the other girl, the lace which lined her sleeves falling back to disclose her lovely arms.

"Oh, I do think I want your help, Jennie," she whispered, "for indeed I do not know what to do about the note Molly has sent me! I know that she has been the cause of Uncle's becoming ill again and that I should be angry with her, and yet . . ."

"A note!" Jennifer exclaimed. "Come! Show it to me!"

"I have only the pieces here," Susan replied, taking a few scraps of paper from the reticule which she had flung on the sofa when coming into the room. "She wrote that I was to destroy it, you see, as soon as I had read the contents. But you need not try to put the bits together for I remember what she wrote well enough. It seems that she and Alfred . . ."

"Alfred?"

"Lord Bemis's footman. It seems that they are in need of funds before they can carry out their elopement and I am to send them as many guineas as I can muster to the Boar's Head on the north road out of town by this afternoon."

"Why, has the jade taken herself off with someone totally without funds!" Jennifer cried, torn between amusement and horror. "What a choice she has in gentlemen, to be sure!"

"Do not speak so loudly, pray!" Susan begged her. "Besides, that is not the case, for she wrote—I could scarcely make out the scribble—that Alfred would have money enough of his own in a few days for he is a dutiful son, it appears, and sends his wages home to his poor mother every quarter. It is to his mother's house that he is taking Molly, I believe, for she wrote the name of the village, although I could not make out the word."

"I do not like the sound of it," Jennifer replied.

"But surely we cannot stand in the way of true love," Susan declared. "Much as we will hate to lose her, we must not put our own interests first. Uncle, of course, would not understand that, which is why I knew I could not go to him directly."

"I beg you not to be so romantic," Jennifer said. "Pause and think for a moment, do. Do you really believe that Molly can be in love with a fellow she has known such a short time?"

"Time has nothing to do with such matters, I believe," Susan said, flushing and lowering her eyes.

"Well, as for that, perhaps you are right," Jennifer relented. "But there is this to consider. You are as well acquainted as I with Molly's escapades in the past. You know how she allowed herself to be misled then."

"There must always be a first time for someone to be right," Susan said stubbornly. "Even Molly. And besides, does he not sound a good enough fellow?"

"Too good perhaps," Jennifer mused. "So he has

sent his wages home to his mother, has he? And he intends to take Molly to her? No doubt she is a good and honest widow who lives neatly in a cottage covered with roses and she will welcome our dear abigail with open arms and . . . "

"Must you always play the cynic, Jennie?" Susan demanded. "Why should not that be the case exactly?"

"Because the world is what it is," Jennifer said in a low voice. "Come, let us agree to this. We will go together to the Boar's Head and take the money with us. But before we will deliver it to the happy couple, we must have the opportunity of meeting Alfred and forming some decision as to his character."

"I do not like playing judge and jury with other people's lives," Susan murmured.

It was so nearly what she herself had said to Sir John Evans not an hour before that Jennifer was startled into silence. And in that moment a knock sounded at the door and the next moment a harassed-appearing Mrs. Capstone was announcing Lord Bemis.

His lordship was a stout, imposing gentleman with a very red face and a cravat which gave every sign of having been knotted inexpertly.

"I am afraid, sir, that my uncle is indisposed," Jennifer said with all the composure she could muster, "but, since my sister and I are well acquainted with the circumstances which must have brought you here, perhaps you will be content to talk to us."

It did not appear that Lord Bemis was in a mood to be content with anything. Outrage was written in large letters on his broad face, but he allowed himself to be coaxed into a chair and proceeded to hem and haw, all the while knotting and unknotting his fists.

"Do you see this cravat, ladies!" he began at last in an unexpected fashion.

Susan and Jennifer having replied in unison that indeed they did see it, Lord Bemis continued at some length to explain how only Alfred could tie it satisfactorily. Although he was somewhat incoherent, it soon became clear that his footman was indispensable to him in many other ways as well, which was why he allowed him to serve in a double capacity as his valet.

"In a word," he declared after many hundreds of such had been uttered, "the fellow must not be allowed to stay away long. Once he was gone for two weeks at a time and I will not have that happen again."

"He will want his honeymoon, at least," Susan declared in a spirited manner. "Surely you would not deprive him of that!"

"Honeymoon!" Lord Bemis roared. "Oh, I know his honeymoons well enough!"

"Do you mean that he has been married before?" Susan demanded anxiously.

131

"Married! Alfred married! I hope I shall never see the day, for I would have a wealth of pity for the merry chase he would lead a wife."

"But he intends to wed our abigail," Susan protested. "They have eloped, sir. Did you not have the message? Indeed, I thought that the news originally came from you."

"My cook told me the fellow was off and away again, if that is what you mean, Miss, but that does not mean an elopement in the sense you use the word, I assure you. Oh no, I know Alfred better than that! He will take his pleasure and return all hangdog and ready to be forgiven, for the clever scoundrel knows I cannot do without him. And his excuse will be the usual one, no doubt. Some men will take to drink, you know. Go off on their sprees. Only with Alfred a pretty face and not a bottle is his undoing."

"You do not mean to say, sir, that—that Alfred has done this sort of thing before and that marriage is not his intention!" Susan exclaimed.

"I think he has said it quite clearly, Sister," Jennifer said in a low voice. "And may I ask you, sir, is it your footman's habit to depend on the lady of his choice to provide the funds for these expeditions?"

"That is a shrewd observation, Miss," Lord Bemis replied, growing redder by the minute. "I suppose that must mean that your abigail has taken something of value with her. Well, I will make it good. I have done so in the past, and I suppose I will do so many times again in the future."

"Let me ask you one further question before we proceed," Jennifer said evenly. "Is it true that Alfred sends his wages home to his mother in the country?"

"His mother, Miss! His mother! Why, I hope you will not think it indelicate on my part to say that he never knew his mother or his father either. At least that is the story he has told me often enough in the past when he hoped to win my sympathy, and I have no reason to think it is not true. As for sending his wages anywhere, that does not sound like Alfred to me, for he always has plenty to game with, I believe."

"Then I think we know all we need to know of his character," Jennifer replied. "Do you not agree, Susan?"

Sadly Susan bowed her blond head. "Poor Molly," she murmured.

"Oh, I believe that Molly will recover soon enough," Jennifer told her. "And now, Lord Bemis, if you care to go to the Boar's Head just outside the town, I think you will find your footman safe and well, and our abigail besides. We would be indebted to you, sir, if in return for this information you would see that she is safely returned to us."

"Why, bless me, Miss, but you have made an easier matter of it than I supposed," Lord Bemis said, rising heavily. "It is a pleasure indeed to meet such a practical lady, make no mistake on it. No talk of hearts and flowers! No fits of hysterics! Why, Damme, it is enough to make me think my luck is changing as far as Alfred is concerned."

"No hearts and flowers," Jennifer said in a low voice as she closed the door behind him. "I expect he spoke more truly than he knew."

Chapter Eleven

Lord Bemis had no sooner left when Lady Tassing hurried into the room, intent on finding out what had happened.

"La!" she exclaimed when Jennifer had finished with an explanation which lost nothing from being an abbreviated account. "What good fortune that your uncle was not in the room when he arrived. He must never be told, my dear! Never! Why, I declare, I believe his health would not stand the shock."

While she was speaking the door to the Duke of Jennings's bedchamber opened slowly and, although both Jennifer and Susan made frantic gestures to warn Lady Tassing to put an end to her explication, her back being to the door, she appar-

135

ently assumed that they were giving vent to a general nervousness and continued to speak in a penetrating voice.

"Shame alone would produce a relapse," she declared, "for no matter how close-lipped Lord Bemis may be about this affair—and I do not know the gentleman well enough to be certain he *will* be discreet—word will get about, you know. It always does in a place like Bath where everyone knows everyone else's business and . . . "

"I think it delightful that you should take such an interest in Lord Bemis, ma'am!" Jennifer interrupted with an air of desperation, for although she could see nothing of her uncle, she was certain he was listening. "Has he paid you some attention then?"

"Attention?" Lady Tassing exclaimed. "Why, I declare, I would not recognize the gentleman if I were to meet him face to face. If it had not been that Mrs. Capstone chose to mention his visit to you . . . "

"Let us talk of the ball tonight!" Susan cried. "I am thinking of wearing my green and white striped taffeta, but I cannot think how to arrange my hair. Perhaps if you would be good enough to come into my bedchamber, Lady Tassing, and give me some advice while I brush it . . . "

The sound of her uncle clearing his voice in an ominous manner gave her pause. "Now, what is all this I hear about having been paid a visit by a certain Lord Bemis?" he demanded, making a Falstaffian entry, made all the more ungainly by the fact that his left leg sported an enormous bandage as witness to the recurring attack of gout.

Lady Tassing pressed one hand to her lips as Jack lowered his master into his chair and Jennifer and Susan hurried to arrange pillows and footstool with all the frenzy of those intent on distraction.

"Poor Uncle!" Jennifer declared. "I am certain that you need a dose of the new medicine the doctor prescribed. Come, Lady Tassing, Susan, we will go to the chemist to fetch it at once!"

As all three ladies hurried toward the door, the Duke recalled them with a roar which would have struck terror in the heart of a Bengal tiger.

"Not one of you will leave this room until I am possessed with the facts!" he bellowed. "I may be at death's door, but I have not passed through it yet. Damme, do you understand! And now, if you will stop darting around the room like a flock of demented butterflies, I will have an explanation."

"Why," said Jennifer, who was the first to recover her equilibrium, "it is only that Lord Bemis, having heard of your suffering, decided to play the Good Samaritan and . . . "

"He suffers from palpitations like yourself, Uncle," Susan declared earnestly, taking a chair in the further corner of the room and proceeding to tear her handkerchief to shreds.

"Not to mention migraine, sir," Lady Tassing

announced. "Not that they could match yours, of course, but still . . . "

"That is a great deal for *you* to know, ma'am," the Duke announced, "since, as you said, you would not recognize the gentleman if you met him face to face."

"But in Bath everyone knows," Lady Tassing began, and then gave over as the Duke roared again.

"I will have no Banbury tales!" he shouted. "Is that clear to the three of you?"

Silence reigned while all three ladies nodded their heads and assumed the blankest possible expressions.

"And I will not have you tell me that you do not know the answer to my questions," the Duke warned, "the first of which is why Lord Bemis may have occasion to bring shame to me."

Lady Tassing looked at Susan, who looked at Jennifer, who looked at Jack, who shrugged his shoulders helplessly.

"Well, Uncle," Jennifer said wearily, "if you *will* know, Molly attempted to elope with Lord Bemis's footman, a fellow whom, it seems, he cannot spare, despite the fact that the man has often engaged in similar escapades. But," she added hastily as her uncle gripped his cane and began to thump it on the floor in a manner which seemed to bode no good, "there is no need to be concerned, for the footman, being out of funds, was

138

forced to halt at an inn not far from town and is, I think, at this very moment, being interviewed by Lord Bemis, who seemed to have no other thought in mind but that the fellow be returned to his employ at the soonest opportunity. As for Molly . . . "

"I expect you will want to return her to the country, sir," Lady Tassing suggested faintly. "You were quite right of course—as you always are—in saying that she should never have been brought here in the first place. A new abigail can be found for the girls, or perhaps they could share mine with me, for I declare the chit has more time on her hands than . . . "

"Silence!" the Duke declared. "So Molly tried to fly the coop, did she? And with a penniless footman."

"He told her that he had sent all his earnings home to his mother, Uncle," Susan whispered. "No doubt he seemed to Molly to be a good and honest person . . . "

"Like that blacksmith, eh?" the Duke demanded. "And all the other scoundrels who have turned her pretty head over the years. Never a thought of her poor mother did she have then, and not a thought of me now! Damme, the girl's a jade, but I cannot help but admire such persistence. Not to mention consistency! Eye for the wrong ones, she has!"

"But are you not angry, Uncle?" Jennifer asked in amazement.

"Damned glad to have the gel back!" the Duke declared, continuing to thump his cane but rather now as though he were keeping time to music. "Make her tell me all about it! Better than a tonic. Eh? Eh?"

"If you say so, Uncle," Jennifer replied with an air of relief. "Of course, she may be brokenhearted."

"Not our Molly!" the Duke predicted.

And indeed such was not the case, for an hour later the abigail returned in a state of high dudgeon and was still regaling the Duke with the details of her misfortune when Jennifer and Susan joined Lady Tassing on the landing to go to the Assembly Room.

As the carriage rattled down the street, Jennifer put all thought of domestic matters aside. The evening promised little enjoyment for her since she knew that she must take the occasion to explain to Lord Watching why he must not put himself in the awkward position of seeking another interview with her uncle. She had tried to explain something of what she intended to do to Susan while they had been dressing, but the girl seemed averse to speaking seriously on any subject aside from saying in a lighthearted manner, which Jennifer guessed was bravely assumed, that it must be delightful to have a beau like Lord Watching and that she intended to find one herself at the soonest opportunity.

And, as they entered the brilliantly lighted ball-room, Jennifer, glancing at her sister, who was a golden-haired vision in taffeta and lace, guessed that were Susan to be so determined, she would attract many beaux and she could only hope that Lord Watching would soon be one of them.

But first it was necessary to disillusion that gentleman on her own account. And yet, on her first look about the long room, she saw no sight of him. Instead Amelia and Sir John Evans danced past her and something knotted in her throat, for although Sir John apparently did not see her, Amelia raised her fan over his shoulder and fluttered it with an air of triumph.

"The dear girl will flaunt herself so," Lady Daphne said, appearing at Jennifer's elbow. "Strange affair, that. Seemed a sensible gentleman, the few times I've spoken with him. Not the sort to be taken in, do you think?"

"Perhaps Sir John sees her well enough for what she is and likes what he sees," Jennifer said, although the words cost her an effort. "She is very beautiful."

"When you have said that, you have said all," Lady Daphne replied, shaking her head. "My daughter is an artful schemer, Jennie, as well you know. And were Sir John Evans not the sort of intelligent and sensitive gentleman I take him to be, I would think fit to warn him. For you know, do you not, that had it not been for the news of his

141

fortune, she would never have transferred her affections from Lord Watching to him?"

"Perhaps he does not mind my cousin's motives," Jennifer murmured. And at that moment it struck her as certain that she had been used by Sir John to wean Lord Watching away from the very lady he had probably set his cap for on the first instance of seeing her. Yes, that would explain his irritation when she had explained to him that she could take no further part in the deception, although why he had been so bothered about Lord Watching's character she could not guess. Unless, that is, he thought that without her to distract the young man, Lord Watching might become once again a formidable rival for Amelia's affections.

The thought made her all the more determined to carry out her intent. It would serve Sir John well enough if Lord Watching should return to the chase once more. What a fool she had been to allow herself to be the means of his distraction!

"Is your uncle in worse health than usual, my dear?" Lady Daphne inquired. "Take my word on it, he has been a hypochondriac since he was a boy and will probably outlive us all."

"Uncle was in fine spirits when I left him," Jennifer assured her aunt. "I think that you should know—before you hear it from another quarter—that our abigail, Molly . . . "

But she was not allowed time to finish, for at

that moment Lord Watching made his appearance, his face as blandly hopeful as usual, and asked her for the next cotillion.

Taking his arm, Jennifer suggested that she would rather go to one of the quieter anterooms and have a conversation.

"In the first place, sir," she said when they were seated on the window seat together, "I must apologize for my uncle making no reply to your request for an interview, but his health, as you know, is uncertain, and today he suffered a relapse from which, I am happy to say, he is now quite recovered."

"Then I will send another note tomorrow," Lord Watching said with charming simplicity.

"Indeed I do not think you should," Jennifer told him quietly. "How long have we known one another, sir?"

"Why, I believe it is more than a fortnight," the young man replied.

"And do you remember what you told me when we first met?" Jennifer asked him.

"Why, I think I was in a mood of self-pity," he replied. "My new title sat very heavily on me."

"And does it seem less of a burden now?"

"Indeed, I have not given it a thought for a great number of days."

"And why is that, sir?"

"I cannot think why you ask, Miss Damion," he said fondly, attempting to pick up her hand and seeing it escape from him in the direction of her fan. "But I expect it is because of the close friendships I have formed. One closer than the others, I dare to hope."

"Your first close friendship, as you call it, was with my cousin, I believe," Jennifer murmured.

"Ah, but that was a passing fancy," he told her.

"On your part or hers, sir?"

He seemed puzzled for a moment.

"Let me put it another way," Jennifer proposed. "If her attention had not turned to Sir John Evans, what would have been the consequences, do you think? Be honest now, I beg you."

"Why, I have not given it consideration, Miss Damion."

"That is my point exactly," Jennifer told him. "You do not give anything sufficient consideration. Let me be blunter than I meant to be. Why do you suppose my cousin turned to the gentleman in question?"

"I expect she found him more to her liking," Lord Watching replied.

"And did that not affect you, sir?"

"Why, it might have done, had it not been for you, Miss Damion. You were kind enough to show a certain friendship for me . . . "

"A friendship that was meant truly enough," Jennifer told him gently. "But had I not been on hand, and had Sir John not made an appearance, is it not likely that you would have penned a letter to Lady Daphne today rather than to my uncle?"

For a moment he was silent. From the other room the music rose and fell.

"I take your meaning," he said slowly. "What you are saying is that I am easily led. That I do not understand my own emotions."

"I only think that you do not know the meaning of true love," Jennifer told him. "You wish to be liked. There is no harm in that, but in your case there are special circumstances which should make you cautious. Coming, as you did, into a large fortune and a title, you found yourself alienated. You needed desperately to feel that you could be appreciated for yourself alone. Is that not so?"

"Perhaps you are right," he said, his blue eyes intent on hers. "Do you mean that I have been deceived by you, Miss Damion?"

"If I were intent on deception I would not be speaking so honestly with you," she assured him. "But let us face the world as it is. You were wary enough of it when I met you, but when my cousin showed you her attention . . . "

"Do you mean that it was my fortune and my title . . . "

"We cannot be sure otherwise," Jennifer told him. "The fact is that she turned aside soon enough and I do not think it coincidence that this occurred when she heard of Sir John's wealth. But

I do not mean to slander her, sir. I know her well, and I am determined to speak honestly."

"And you, Miss Damion," he said, his face grown pale, "do you mean to tell me in this indirect fashion that you have found someone with a greater title or greater wealth?"

"Indeed I do not!" Jennifer cried. "I have no wish to make a cynic of you, sir. Better far that you retain your innocence. But you cannot be one day enamored with my cousin and the next with me. That is the crux of the matter!"

Lord Watching stared at her earnestly.

"You mean to say that I am fickle?" he muttered.

"That is a lady's role," Jennifer assured him with a smile. "I have no doubt that you think yourself sincere. But we are scarcely more than acquaintances, sir. You do not truly know me, just as you did not know Amelia. I would only hope that in the future you would take the time to know for certain in what direction your heart lies. For you have a heart, sir, although at present it has not been touched."

"We are no more than acquaintances?" he said helplessly, as though he could not take her meaning.

"No, I was wrong in that," Jennifer told him. "We are friends, sir. And always will be if I have any say in the matter. Is my advice to you so unendurable?"

"Indeed, I think you speak to a point," Lord Watching told her. "And that is that we may be mistaken . . ."

Glancing through the doorway Jennifer saw Sir John and Amelia whirl past. Her cousin's eyes were aglow and Sir John was laughing.

"You are not the only one to be mistaken," she assured the young man at her side. "I would not have you hurt as I . . ."

"As you, Miss Damion?"

"It was nothing," she assured him brightly. "And now, perhaps, we can wait together for the next cotillion."

Chapter Twelve

"I liked the old gaffer better when he was always threatening me," Molly declared with fervor, clutching her mob cap with both hands and pulling it down until it completely covered her lovely curls.

"How often have I told you that the Duke is not to be referred to as 'the old gaffer'?" Jennifer reproved the abigail, but she spoke gently since, despite Molly's attempt at bravado, she guessed that the girl felt the hurt of deceit as much as anyone placed in a like situation might do. "And as for his threatening you, I should think you would be glad to have him leave off."

"It's only that his lordship thinks of me as a bottle of medicine," Molly protested. "I declare that I never thought to see the day I would replace his hartshorn. And I'll tell you this," she added in a whisper, "if he thinks I'm always at his beck and call, he must think again, for I've still a plan or two up my sleeves. I won't be leaving Bath without a ring on my finger. Wait and see."

"Indeed I hope you do find someone suitable, Molly," Jennifer said wearily. As usual when she had suggested that the gowns be sorted and a general tidying up should take place, she had discovered that it was she who did most of the work while Molly perched on the side of the bed and talked.

Shaking out a petticoat and folding it, she considered that there were other causes for the particular languor she seemed to suffer this morning. Susan had insisted on sitting up half the night discussing the gentlemen she had met at the ball in a voice which was too brightly artificial to deceive Jennifer, who knew that her sister had been put out when Lord Watching had left the Assembly Room directly after dancing the one cotillion, and she had not felt that in all decency she could explain. Then, too, there was the matter of Sir John Evans and Amelia. She did not know why the thought of them together should prey on her so, for after all, he was a man of the world, well able to look after himself.

"And what do you think of that, Miss?" she

heard Molly demand. "I expect I've shocked you, haven't I?"

"I'm sorry," Jennifer replied, "but my mind was wandering. Do you expect you could attend to this rip in my sister's pink silk while you repeat whatever it was that is supposed to shock me?"

"Why, you know, Miss, I'm not one to talk and work at the same time," Molly replied pertly. It was plain to Jennifer that the abigail had taken the Duke's newfound dependence on her to indicate that she could neglect her other duties with impunity. With pursed lips, she went to fetch the sewing basket from its corner and handed it to Molly along with the gown in question.

"Then you must work in silence, I suppose," she said.

"I expect I could try to do both," Molly declared sullenly, "for I think it only right that I should warn you, Miss, that you will soon have to be looking for someone to take my place."

It occurred to Jennifer to retort that given the amount of work Molly did not do, she would scarcely need a replacement, but she reminded herself that she had promised to be kind, no matter how sorely her temper might be tried.

"And do you mean to leave us directly?" she inquired.

Molly gave up her feeble attempt to thread a needle. "Why, if you had been listening, Miss, you would have heard me say that I do not intend to find someone suitable. Suitable is for the Quality like you and Miss Susan. Alfred was my choice yesterday and he'll be my choice tomorrow, even though he did play me for a gudgeon."

"Have a care with your language, Molly," Jennifer said more out of habit than conviction.

"Well, it's the only way I know to put it, Miss, and that's a fact. He may have thought he could deceive me with all his talk about an old mother and the rest but I guessed at the truth soon as he told me he was out of funds. I know the way of the world, Miss, as well as anyone about."

"I should have thought you might," Jennifer said in a low voice, setting about the slippers Susan had worn the night before with a brush. "But all that aside, do you mean to say you intended to have him compromise you?"

"Indeed I did, Miss!" Molly said with enthusiasm, "and if you and Miss Susan hadn't played the tipstaff with Lord Bemis, I'd have been a fallen woman by today."

"It seems an odd ambition," Jennifer said dryly, "but I am certain you had your reasons."

"Why, I'd have had him before the law if he hadn't married me after," Molly declared. "I only wanted the chance to show him I'm not the sort of gel he's gone off with in the past."

"That shows a certain enterprise on your part," Jennifer replied, turning her head so that Molly would not see her smile. "But are you quite cer-

151

tain that it would all have been worth the effort?"

"Oh, it would have been no effort, Miss," the abigail declared. "At least not the first part of it. If you had ever seen Alfred you would not have had to ask. A Greek god, Miss, that's what he is, a perfect Apple."

"I expect you mean Apollo," Jennifer suggested. "But handsome is as handsome does, they say, and given Alfred's reputation . . . "

"I never wanted a fellow without a reputation, Miss!" Molly exclaimed. "Why, you can never guess what dull chaps most of these footmen are. No, it's Alfred as takes my fancy, and I shall have him in the end for I have a plan."

"I hope it is better than the first one," Jennifer said. "Come, can I help you thread that needle?"

"If you like, Miss, but as to what we were speaking of. There are plans and plans, you know. Surely you have made them yourself. And when one fails, there is always another at hand. After all, a body cannot simply sit back and let life bring what it may. Why, left to itself, life is not to be depended on."

"You rival Plato as a philosopher," Jennifer told her. "But were you to take my advice, you would not try too hard to manipulate, for that can bring a deal of trouble, I assure you."

"You have the sound of someone whose own plans have gone sour, Miss," Molly said pertly.

"I think we have had enough of conversation

for this morning," Jennifer replied more sharply than she intended. And leaving the abigail to her uncertain labor, she went into the sitting room, hoping to find a moment of quiet. But in this she was to be disappointed, for Lady Tassing had descended on her uncle at the moment of his return from the baths, and was holding him captive in his chair.

"I was just telling your uncle, Jennie," her ladyship declared, "that the best medicine in the world for him would be to accompany me to the Pump Room."

"Damme, I can do quite well here listening to Molly!" the Duke replied stubbornly. "What have I to do with Pump Rooms? Send the gel to me, Jennifer."

"Molly is occupied at present in what should be her natural duties," his niece replied. "Had it not been for the fact that I am forced to make her attend to her work, I would have been able to accompany Susan this morning. As it is, she is strolling on the Crescent with a certain Marquess she met last evening, and although she told me his mother would be in attendance, I have reason to think . . . "

"You cannot think she is with the Marquess of Kelso!" Lady Tassing exclaimed. "Why, I saw that she took to the dance floor twice with him last night, but I scarcely thought that . . . "

"What is wrong with Lord Kelso?" the Duke demanded, pounding the floor with his cane.

"If you had been in as constant attendance at the Pump Room as I," Lady Tassing declared, "you would have no need to ask. The fellow is the worst kind of dandy with his eye out for any heiress who comes into view."

"How is it then that Molly has never mentioned him?" the Duke demanded.

"You must understand, sir," Lady Tassing said patiently, "that Molly is in possession of only a limited amount of gossip. But at the Pump Room . . . "

"Do you mean that there are more follies to be heard of?" the Duke bellowed. "More reputations to be torn to shreds?"

"You cannot know one half of the scandal which Bath provides if you insist on remaining here in this room and listening to the tattle of a servant," Lady Tassing said quite sternly. "Is that not so, Jennie?"

Turning, she winked so broadly that Jennifer was forced to agree. Only moments before Molly had spoken of plans and it seemed clear that, having discovered that the Duke had an insatiable thirst for gossip, a thirst strong enough to divert him from his medicine, Lady Tassing had decided to act on the fact.

"The Pump Room is a beehive of gossip, Uncle," the girl assured him. "I expect it might be too much for you."

The challenge was all that was needed, for already the Duke was out of his chair and, forgetting to limp, proceeding in a determined fashion to his chamber. With a promise that he would be ready in a few minutes, he disappeared and Lady Tassing rushed to embrace Jennifer.

"What an extraordinary man your uncle is, my dear!" she cried. "Only think how bravely he forgets his pain in order to accompany me to the Pump Room. Why, I never thought I would see the day! Bath has brought all manner of change to him, has it not? And as for the Marquess of Kelso, if Susan is indeed with him, it does not matter whether his mother is in their company or not, for I confess to having fibbed a bit to accomplish my purpose. Indeed, I can say nothing worse about the gentleman than that he is a simpering idiot."

That was some comfort to Jennifer, but not enough, for as she bid farewell to her uncle, remarkably spruce in a blue frock coat and tan breeches and watched from the window as he handed Lady Tassing into her carriage, she considered that if Lord Watching did not happen to turn his attention to Susan, her sister might deceive herself into thinking that even a simpering idiot was better than nothing.

However, despite Molly's lecture on the value of plans, Jennifer could not see that there was anything she could do to curb Susan's impulses. If she were to tell her sister how she and Sir John Evans had connived to keep Lord Watching from following his fancy, she would only succeed in painting the gentleman she believed her sister loved in colors which would do nothing but serve as disillusionment. If the day did come when he saw fit to pay Susan some attention, she would only mistrust it. And, believing, as she did, that the two eminently suited one another, Jennifer was not willing to say anything which might put Susan off.

What she wanted, she saw quite clearly, was some way to manipulate her sister's happiness. And yet after what she had said to Sir John Evans on the subject, how could she think of such a thing? What right had she to meddle with anyone? She, who could not even plot her own course to happiness!

These musings led to a pensive mood which Amelia interrupted, bursting into the sitting room without even a tap at the door to announce her, her mother following in her wake as one who braves the rapids.

"Can you imagine!" Amelia began without prelude. "The gentleman has made a fool of me and I declare it was all your doing, Jennifer!"

"Calm yourself, Amelia, do!" Lady Daphne declared, sinking onto the sofa and proceeding to wave her fan in every imaginable direction. "Remember that your cousin has not a clue as to what you are talking about."

Amelia took a position in the center of the room. Despite the stylish cut of her sarsenet walking dress, not to mention her bonnet with upstanding poke and ostrich plumes, she could have been Medea vowing vengeance to the gods.

"The gentleman will be sorry that he ever trifled with me!" she declared. "The word will be all over Bath before the day is finished if I have any way with it, and then let him find another young lady of fortune to make sport of!"

"You speak of Sir John Evans, I presume," Jennifer said evenly.

"The name will never pass my lips again!" Amelia assured her passionately. "Heir to a great fortune, is he? Houses in the country? A place in London?"

"But surely he never spoke of such to you," Jennifer protested. "Nor did I, Cousin, since you seem to see it fit to blame me as well as him."

"Someone set the rumor about!" Amelia declared. "And I think it might as well have been you, for the end result was that I allowed Lord Watching to transfer his affections, did I not?"

"Lord Watching is no more than a friend to me and never has been!" Jennifer declared with rising anger.

"La, la!" Lady Daphne exclaimed. "What a to-do this is, I declare."

"It will be no to-do, Aunt," Jennifer assured her, "if your daughter will watch her words, for, I assure you, I am in no mood to bear the brunt of her anger. Particularly since I do not know what has happened."

"I should have thought it would be easy enough for someone as clever as you to guess," Amelia sneered. "I have heard the truth. The gentleman is a mere knight with nothing to his name but a ramshackle country estate."

"And how heard you this?" Jennifer inquired with attention.

For the first time since she had arrived, Amelia seemed flustered.

"He—he told me himself," she said in a low voice. "Just at the moment when I thought he was to declare himself, he confessed the truth."

"And what brought him to the subject, pray?" Jennifer demanded.

"My daughter, fond as always of anticipating, was going on about how much she enjoyed luxury, I believe," Lady Daphne said tartly.

"I only happened to mention how convenient it would be to have a town house in London and a number of country residences as well," Amelia pouted.

"And Sir John . . . "

"He replied that he thought it might serve very well for some people, but that for himself he was content with his own small manor house which, although in a state of considerable disrepair . . . ”

With a cry, Amelia threw herself against a convenient wall and began to drum the plaster with such vigor that several pictures fell to the floor.

“Calm yourself!” Jennifer demanded, going to her cousin and taking her by her shoulders. “Tell me this. Had Sir John ever told you himself that he possessed vast estates?”

“No!” Amelia gasped. “No, he did not! But it is common knowledge. He must have put the rumor about himself! The scoundrel! And to think that I gave up Lord Watching for such a man!”

“You accuse Sir John of deceit,” Jennifer said, forcing her cousin to face her. “And yet have you not been guilty of something worse?”

“Ah, Jennifer, I knew I could depend on you to put the matter in perspective,” Lady Daphne cried, throwing her fan to the floor.

“There is nothing worse than deceit!” Amelia cried.

“I think there is, and I think as well that you know it,” Jennifer told her. “You pretended to be fond of Lord Watching until it did not seem to suit your interest. And then you played the flirt with Sir John for no better reason than that you thought him a more lucrative prize. If you have been disappointed, it is no more than you deserve. Spiders weave their webs from necessity. You wove yours out of simple greed. If you seek to blame someone, blame yourself."

"How well you put things, Niece!" Lady Daphne declared. "Come, Amelia! Let us be off. No doubt you will wish to consult your list."

With a cry of outrage, Amelia dashed out the door and Lady Daphne, pausing to embrace Jennifer, said simply, "It was a plan, was it not?"

"Yes," Jennifer admitted, tears coming to her eyes as she felt her aunt's soft cheek against hers. "And I am sorry for it."

"But I am not," Lady Daphne told her. "I have waited nineteen years to see Amelia put in her place. Only think of this, my dear. In the end, you and Sir John may have done her a great favor."

But Jennifer was not so certain. As soon as her aunt had taken her departure, she banished Molly from the still untidy bedchamber and threw herself across the bed, a prey to disquieting emotions she could not wholly understand.

Chapter Thirteen

That same day Jennifer heard from Lady Tassing that Sir John Evans had left Bath for London and that the Pump Room was seething with rumors that the cause of his departure was the fact that he had offered for Amelia and been rejected.

"Indeed, the gel indicated that something of the sort might be true when she and her mother joined the company just before your uncle and I took our departure," Lady Tassing went on, "for she colored ever so prettily when she heard his name mentioned and begged Lady Youster, who begged to know the truth, not to mention the gentleman since, in all truth, she wished to say nothing which might prove an embarrassment to the gentleman."

"More than likely the fellow gave her the slip," the Duke muttered, disengaging Lady Tassing's arm from his and sinking into his chair with a groan. "Seemed a sensible chap to me the one time we held a conversation, and what a sensible chap would want with my niece I'll be dashed if I know."

It was all that Jennifer could do not to tell him that he had guessed the truth, more or less, but she bethought herself that what Amelia had told her had been said in confidence, and that if her cousin wished to keep her pride by allowing false rumors to circulate it was her business. Besides, by his abrupt and unannounced departure Sir John had clearly made it evident that he wished for no defenders. Having played a role to his own satisfaction, he had probably found himself bored and was even now seeking new manipulations of the sort which seemed to intrigue him in London.

Assuring herself that she would not give the gentleman another thought, Jennifer asked her uncle if he had enjoyed his expedition, thus eliciting such a flood of scandal, most of it concerning people she had never met, that she eagerly took the excuse of Susan's flushed return to escape the sitting room, leaving Lady Tassing and her uncle to continue their discussion of the foibles of Bath society in private.

"I think I liked Uncle better when nothing concerned him more than his health," Susan said petulantly, throwing her bonnet on the bed. "At least I did not expect to return home to replace one boring conversation for another."

"Was it Lord Kelso's mother who was so tiresome then?" Jennifer asked her sister, aware at the moment of putting the question that she was strangely no more interested in the answer than she had been in her uncle's metamorphosis from hypochondriac to scandalmonger.

"I declare, one was as dull as the other!" Susan exclaimed. "Of course, I expect I have nothing more to look forward to if I persist in making comparisons."

"Do you mean that while you were with Lord Kelso you thought of another gentleman?" Jennifer asked, her interest quickening since here, at last, was her opportunity to tell her sister that she no longer intended to make herself Lord Watching's companion.

Susan flushed. "How cruel of you, Jennie!" she exclaimed. "You know full well that I am only looking hither and thither because of you."

"It is not like you to be so oblique," Jennifer reminded her. "Can we not speak plainly?"

"I see no need to do so under the circumstances," Susan reminded her. "You have chosen your beau and Amelia has hers."

"Ah, but that is where you are wrong," Jennifer told her sister eagerly. "You, at least, should know the truth, which is that Amelia has discovered that

Sir John Evans does not possess the wealth she thought and has discontinued her interest in him accordingly. Indeed, the gentleman has gone to London."

It was strange that the announcement caused her to flush, but so it did and it was necessary for her to turn away from Susan until her face had stopped burning.

"As for Lord Watching," Jennifer went on in an even voice, "we are no more than friends and never will be."

There was no time for her to observe her sister's reaction to that bit of information since, at the moment she made it, the curtains which partly concealed the window seat began to rustle and a disheveled Molly emerged, rubbing her eyes with one hand and holding the gown she was supposed to have mended in the other.

"There, now, a nap has done me good!" the abigail declared, dropping the garment to the floor and stretching in her usual unselfconscious manner. "The fact is that I had a dream which I take as a good omen. I declare that Alfred must see to himself, for I believe I have such a scheme . . . But, la! I suppose the old gaffer—begging your pardon, His Lordship—must be waiting for me to give him his daily dose of news."

"I believe you will find that my uncle has found another source of information," Jennifer told the abigail dryly. "But your release from one sort of duty does not absolve you from the others, and I would take it kindly if you would remove yourself and this gown, together with the sewing basket, to your room upstairs and set about a task which should have been finished hours ago."

Grumbling, Molly took her departure and Jennifer turned her attention to her sister who, rather than seeming pleased that Lord Watching was not spoken for, seemed oddly uncommunicative, going so far as to plead a migraine, which affliction, never having visited her before, could only lead Jennifer to guess that Susan wished to be alone.

Feeling strangely at a loss, she retreated to the sitting room, only to find that Molly had joined her uncle and Lady Tassing and was lending her comments and observations to their tittle-tattle with an enthusiasm which caused Jennifer to collect her pelisse and leave the room unobserved, with some vague intention of walking to the lending library.

But, indeed, she forgot her purpose as soon as she reached the street and found herself wandering blindly in the direction of the Crescent, lost in thought.

How strange a thing it was to find herself unneeded. For as long as she could remember her uncle had depended on her to listen to his recital of various ailments and, tiresome though that had been, she realized now that it had given her life some direction. And then there was Susan, who had always been so open and loving to her, a Susan who apparently preferred to keep her own council now. More recently there had been Molly's behavior to concern her, and yet even she now seemed determined to take her affairs in hand in a manner which, although it might not prove responsible, reflected a certain assurance which Jennifer found daunting. There was not even any need for herself to concern herself with Lord Watching's future, since she had voluntarily given over the manipulation of it. And as for Sir John . . . Of him she would not even think. Passing a narrow-paned shop window, Jennifer paused to look at her own reflection as though to assure herself that she was really there.

The sense of desolation continued through that day and the next and it was only on the occasion of the next ball held at the Assembly Room that Jennifer roused herself at Lady Tassing's urgings to make the fourth member of the company.

"Can you believe that your uncle has consented to attend?" the older woman asked her. "I declare, I am as flustered as a gel, although I know well enough that he has only agreed to accompany me because I assured him that to observe the follies of society at firsthand was preferable to simply hearing them discussed the next morning at the Pump Room. I believe I will wear my new scarlet gown and turban in honor of the occasion! Do you expect he will go so far as to take to the dance floor with me? La, but you must go with us, child, for if you do not I will feel myself constantly distracted by keeping watch on Susan. And I do believe she needs a watching, for I think she has been behaving rather strangely of late."

Since it was true that Susan had continued to keep to herself, and that Jennifer was aware of how important it was to Lady Tassing that she be free to center all of her attention on the Duke on this, his first foray into formal society, Jennifer agreed to accompany them, although her heart was not in it and, as a result, she found herself entering the now familiar ballroom with her uncle, looking quite the dandy in his new evening clothes with, his wig discarded, his grizzled hair arranged in something which approximated the new Brutus cut, followed by Susan, a vision in pale blue satin, and Lady Tassing, who swept across the floor like a triumphant scarlet meteor.

How rapidly the company dissolved, for Lady Tassing was intent on introducing the Duke to as many of the objects of their scandalmongering as possible, while Lord Watching, bland-faced and smiling as always, after a hesitant glance at Jennifer, who shook her head, asked Susan to join him in a waltz.

There was some pleasure in that, at least, Jennifer found, for having refused three offers to take to the floor, she placed herself in such a situation as to allow her to see that Susan was all aglow and that, when the music ceased, Lord Watching was to be seen in animated conversation with her sister and that the next waltz found them on the dance floor again.

But the comfort the sight gave her was short-lasting. The second waltz being over, she observed Lord Watching on his way to fetch some punch for himself and her sister, only to be intercepted, before he had taken seven steps, by Amelia, a glittering figure in blue damask embroidered with gold figures, who descended on him like a veritable Diana only lacking the quiver and arrows.

In despair Jennifer saw that gentleman diverted from his course toward the punch bowl. Amelia's smile glittered. She was all animation. He could not have subtracted himself from her had he tried. And he did for a moment seem to try. Jennifer saw him give a backward look at Susan, who had, unfortunately or not, been surrounded by the very sort of fop and dandy which make a habit of filling vacuums created around young ladies of an innocent nature.

Jennifer started toward her sister just at the moment the orchestra struck up the opening notes of a cotillion. Glancing toward the dance floor, she saw her uncle taking his position opposite Lady Tassing in the line, for all the world as though he had never heard of gout. For a moment the extraordinary sight distracted her and when she turned back to where Susan had been standing with her admirers, it was just in time to see a familiar figure bow to her sister and present his arm. And, in a moment, Susan and Sir John Evans stood facing one another on the dance floor.

Chapter Fourteen

"I declare I was as surprised to see him as anyone," Susan said the next morning as Jennifer
helped her with the back buttons of her sprigged
muslin gown, "for of course I knew he had gone to
London. But he replied that business had taken
him there and curiosity had brought him back,
whatever that was meant to mean. He is a strange
sort of gentleman, though charming enough, I'm
sure. But then I do not need to tell you that."

"You may tell me anything about him that you
care to and I will be prepared to believe it," Jennifer
said dryly.

Her sister turned to embrace her in the old way.

"Oh, Jennie, I have been such a nuisance to you

170

these past few days!" she cried. "And now I am afraid that you are angry with me."

"Why should I be angry?" Jennifer replied. "I assure you I am delighted to see you in such a good humor."

"Then why is there something in your voice which hints at annoyance?" Susan asked her. "No, wait a moment, do! We need not join Uncle just yet. Indeed, I would be as glad if we did not join him for breakfast now but waited until he goes to the baths, for then we could have a cozy chat together and . . ."

"He expects us to join him," Jennifer reminded her. "Do you not hear his cane on the floor?"

"Oh, but I do not know what to make of Uncle now," Susan whispered. "Did you not notice the way in which he pranced about the floor last night? Quite as though he had never suffered a day's illness in his life. And Lady Tassing was as gay as a gel at her first ball! Until the last waltz, that is. Who *was* that lady Uncle was dancing with, do you know? Such a strange orange turban as she was wearing and her ways were *that* arch, I'm sure. I asked Lady Tassing about her on the landing when we returned home last night, but she was in a pet of some sort and went off without a word."

The cane's beat, which had begun as a pulse, now sounded like a hammer.

171

"There is no making him wait," Jennifer murmured. "Come along, do! Things are at fours and sixes enough without Uncle losing his temper to boot."

"Well, Miss!" the Duke exclaimed as Susan took her seat at the table which he had had set up, as usual, at the convenient distance from his easy chair. "You have made a conquest, I see, and I declare it meets with my approval."

"I declare, I do not know what you mean, Uncle," Susan said, flushing modestly.

"Fine piece of ham!" the Duke announced. "I recommend it. And you, Jennie! Make a meal of it for you look a bit pale to me, which comes of being too particular."

"I am never particular about food, Uncle," Jennifer assured him, pouring herself a cup of tea and looking at the ham with distaste.

"I am speaking of gentlemen, gel!" he thundered. "Gentlemen! You should know the meaning of the word, I think, for you turned enough of them away last night."

"I was not in a mood for dancing, sir," Jennifer said shortly.

"Well, Damme, I made up for that, did I not, eh?" the Duke replied. "And so did your sister. What is the fellow's name? Met him once here in this room, as I recall. Expert on diseases, as I recall. Admirable chap! First water!"

"I think you must mean Sir John Evans, Uncle," Susan said in a low voice.

"Kept you to himself, didn't he?" the Duke demanded. "Oh, I kept a sharp eye out! Saw him keep any number of fellows away from you. Must be serious! Bound to be! Even put that chap Amelia was following about out of contention, I noticed."

"That was Lord Watching, Uncle," Jennifer said, buttering a roll and then quite promptly putting it away from her. "Both Sir John and Lord Watching are friends of ours, as Lady Tassing must have told you, and it would do as well to call them by their proper names."

"Hoity-toity, Miss!" the Duke declared. "Something has put you out of temper, I declare. I am not quite the gudgeon you suppose me to be. I keep my ears open. Eh? Eh? Evans was the name of the fellow Amelia had placed her hopes on, I think, and as for Watching, he wrote to ask me for an interview only a week or so ago, I think and it was you, Miss, who asked me not to grant it. There's a mystery here, I think."

"No mystery, Uncle," Jennifer assured him. "Lord Watching was mistaken for a brief while as to whom the object of his affection might be and . . ."

"I did not know that he had asked to speak to

173

Uncle about you, Jennie!" Susan exclaimed, growing pale.

"Nothing came of it," Jennifer assured her. "Lord Watching and I are nothing but friends."

"Are you—are you quite certain?"

"Quite certain," Jennifer said, lightly touching her sister's hand.

"Well, then, what do we care for Watching, eh?" the Duke declared, helping himself to another piece of ham. "Evans is the man we ought to think of. Threw your cousin over, did he? Clever fellow!"

"In the sake of accuracy, Uncle," Jennifer said wearily, "he did not precisely 'throw her over,' as you are good enough to put it. Amelia discovered that he did not have the fortune she thought and returned her attention to Lord Watching as a consequence."

"Amelia always was the practical sort," the Duke said cheerfully, "although her mother calls it by another name. No matter! There is no need for you to play the fortune hunter, Susan. Damme, but I'll be glad enough to have you affianced to a chap who knows a thing or two about medicine. Wouldn't do to have a doctor in the family, of course. All quacks! But add a title . . . "

"I do not intend to be affianced to Sir John, Uncle!" Susan said, starting up from the table. "He was good enough to pay me some attention at

174

the ball, but I think it must have been only kindness on his part. Indeed, since he had never shown me any attention before, I do not know what to make of it."

"Gels would do as well not to think too much," the Duke assured her. "As I was saying to Lady Flauntington last night . . . "

"Was she the person in the orange turban, Uncle?" Jennifer said, relieved beyond words to have the subject turned since perhaps it might keep her, as well as Susan, from wondering about Sir John's motives.

"Couldn't help from noticing her, could you?" the Duke declared in delight. "Splendid lady! Splendid! Perfect mine of information! Knows everything she ought to know and some things that she shouldn't. Eh, Lady Tassing? Eh?"

Apparently they had missed the tap on the door and their friend had let herself in. Jennifer was sorry enough for it when she saw the stricken look on Lady Tassing's face.

"Off to meet her at the Pump Room," the Duke continued, rising to his feet with an alacrity Jennifer had rarely seen him show before. "Jack! Dash it, where's the fellow? Ah, there you are! Gloves! Hat! Is the carriage waiting!"

Lady Tassing did not say a word until the Duke had left the room and then she sank into a chair and requested a cup of tea in a faint voice.

"I am sorry to see Uncle behave in such a fashion," Jennifer told her gently. "How strange it is to see him dash about so. He ought to show more gratitude to you for introducing him to society."

"Who is this Lady Flauntington?" Susan demanded.

"Aside, that is, from being a scandalmonger of the first water," Jennifer added by way of consolation.

"Is she a widow?" Susan asked, handing Lady Tassing a cup of tea.

"Is she quite respectable?" Jennifer added.

"Oh dear, I am afraid she is neither!" Lady Tassing cried, putting aside the tea and wiping her eyes with the edge of the wide sleeve of her yellow morning gown. "The fact is that she is separated from her husband, the Marquess, and that quite against his wishes, I believe. I hear he has followed her to Bath, and that he is a man of quite a violent temper. I do not dare to think what may happen if he sees your uncle consorting with her!"

"But this is terrible!" Susan exclaimed. "Does Uncle know?"

"He fancies himself such a dandy now, that I would not presume to advise him," Lady Tassing said stiffly, regaining her self-possession.

"But what will come of it?" Susan demanded. "La, Jennifer, I think that we should follow him to the Pump Room and make some explanation."

"In the mood he is in, I do not think Uncle would take that kindly," her sister said dryly. "No doubt he will find out his mistake soon enough."

"I would not be so sure of that," Lady Tassing declared, "for I have never seen such a change in a person. I declare, I liked him better when he was a victim of his imagination. Better to have him mourning over a gouty leg than making a fool of himself with Lady Flauntington in public. But then it is none of my affair, and I was a fool ever to think it. I should never have come here, indeed I should not, and I think it best if I return to the country at once."

"But what if Uncle should need you?" Jennifer said in a low voice. "Do not be hasty, I pray you."

"He has never needed me in the past, and I do not think he will need me in the future," Lady Tassing said, rising with all the self-possession she could command and making an uncertain way toward the door.

"Do wait!" Susan cried, running after her.

"Yes, wait and consider for a moment," Jennifer said, following.

So it was that the two girls were standing with their arms about a weeping Lady Tassing when a knock sounded and Mrs. Capstone appeared, one eye aslant as ever, to announce Sir John Evans.

Jennifer's first impulse was to pass him with a nod and escort Lady Tassing to her rooms, but he

177

entered with such an air of assurance and offered a greeting to Lady Tassing with such an air of concern as her appearance demanded that the atmosphere changed of a sudden, and within minutes, all were seated and he was listening to Susan's tale of her Uncle's perfidy with attention.

"Do you think I was wrong not to have warned him, sir?" Lady Tassing demanded.

"A gentleman of his age must make his own mistakes," Sir John replied seriously enough, although Jennifer thought she detected some sign of amusement in his dark eyes. "From what I noticed of him last night, his leg, at least, has taken a decided turn for the better and that is the first thing, surely."

"I trust your judgment, sir," Lady Tassing said with a sigh, "although I do not care to think what may happen if Lord Flauntington finds them together."

"Why, they are in a public place, ma'am, and even if the husband decides to make a nuisance of himself, no doubt the Duke will find a way to cope," he told her. "Indeed, the gentleman struck me as a man of considerable presence the one time we spoke. Besides, one distraction is as good as another, and an angry husband may do him more good than any number of pills."

Jennifer could not think what he was about, but her sister and Lady Tassing had, apparently, no such reservation, for when he suggested that they make him company in his curricle for a drive about town, they both agreed with some enthusiasm.

"We will be seen by everyone," Susan declared in her old ingenuous way.

"If it pleases you, we shall," Sir John said solemnly.

"I would not like the Duke to think I am sitting home moping," Lady Tassing announced. "Yes, it is a splendid idea. I think! I will just go upstairs to fetch my bonnet!"

"And I will fetch mine as well!" Susan declared, hurrying into the other room.

"And will you not accompany us, Miss Damion?" Sir John said slowly when they were alone.

"I think not, sir," Jennifer said in a low voice.

"Ah, I had forgotten how much you dislike manipulation," he replied.

"And is that what you are about, sir?"

"You deceive yourself if you think that there is any other alternative in life," he said quite seriously, his dark eyes on her own. "One may manipulate or be manipulated. That is the only choice."

"I am glad I do not share your philosophy," Jennifer told him.

"You think it wrong then. Perhaps, Miss Damion, if that is indeed the case, you will give me another alternative."

"I will say this and nothing more," Jennifer told

him. "Do not turn my sister's head unless you do it in all honesty."

"If she is clear as to the object of her affections, I do not think her head can be turned," he told her.

"Then you know how she feels about Lord Watching, sir?"

"Do not speak of Watching to me!" he said with some energy. "I saw how he behaved at the Assembly Room yesterday evening as well as you."

"Amelia put him in a position where he could do no other than he did," Jennifer protested.

"So you are still set on defending him."

"I am set on nothing!" Jennifer said impatiently. "But I think you are unfair. He would have returned to Susan had you allowed it. And I mistrust your motives, sir!"

"We must speak of this another time," Sir John said in a low voice as Susan reentered the room by one door and Lady Tassing by the other.

"I think there is no need to anticipate such a discussion, sir," Jennifer said evenly.

"But surely you intend to come with us, Jennie!" Susan cried.

"I believe someone must remain to receive a visitor," Lady Tassing said, "for I saw Mrs. Capstone admitting Lord Watching when I came down the stairs."

For a moment Susan seemed to hesitate. And then, taking Sir John's arm, she made for the door with great determination and passed Lord Watching on the landing with all the aplomb of a seasoned flirt, leaving Jennifer to deal with their unexpected guest as she best could.

Chapter Fifteen

"It is clear that your sister is annoyed with me," Lord Watching said as soon as he had relieved himself of his beaver hat and was sitting opposite Susan on one of the two wing chairs drawn close to the window. "Indeed, I cannot blame her since my behavior toward her at the Assembly Room last evening must have appeared boorish at the very least."

He looked so downcast that Jennifer could not be impatient at him for having arrived unannounced at such an awkward moment. As usual, despite the smartness of his clothes, he had a certain bewildered aspect to him, like a lost child, and she found herself recollecting the confession he had made to her on the occasion of their first meeting. Nothing that he could do then seemed right to him and she could only guess that recent events could have scarcely given him any more faith in himself.

"I came to make an explanation and an apology to her," he continued dolefully, "but since it is quite clear that she is otherwise occupied I must hope that you . . . "

"If an apology is needed, sir," Jennifer said with quiet firmness, "I cannot think but what my sister would appreciate hearing it from your own lips at another time."

"Indeed, I do not know how to put it even to you, Miss Damion," he replied helplessly.

"Why, there should be no trouble in that, sir, if you simply make an honest explanation."

"You know that I left her after our dance with a promise to return with some refreshment?"

"She has said nothing of the matter to me, sir," Jennifer said truthfully. Disturbing as her brief conversation with Sir John had been, she found it possible to put it out of her mind for the present and concentrate, instead, on helping Lord Watching to make an open assessment of the facts. If he could accomplish that in private with herself, no doubt he would be in a better position to be honest with himself in the future. The word "manipulation" came to her mind, but she pushed it away impatiently. Was she not, after all, only doing what any friend would do for another?

"Well, that was what happened," he said in a stumbling manner, "and it was my intention to return, I assure you, but as it happened . . . "

"Yes," Jennifer encouraged him.

"As it happened . . . But I do not wish to seem to be a cad, Miss Damion. Let me only say that a chance encounter . . . "

"If this is to be the manner of your apology to my sister, sir," Jennifer said in a low voice, "I declare, I do not think you ought to make it after all."

"No need to mention names," he muttered as though he were talking to himself. "Very well, then, a certain lady whom I met on the way to the punch table seemed to be under the impression that she had promised the next dance to me, although how she could have made such an error, given the fact that not a word had passed between us that evening, I do not know."

"This lady is the sort to make such a mistake as to promises, I expect," Jennifer murmured.

"Why no, she is not, Miss Damion, and therein lies the puzzle," he replied, as downcast as a boy.

"You have given the matter some thought since, no doubt," Jennifer nudged him. "If mistakes are not the lady's forte, then perhaps another explanation has occurred to you."

"There is the possibility that she is a flirt," he said in a voice which was barely audible.

"And was that the first hint you had that such might be the case?" Jennifer persisted.

"I expect it was not," he confessed. "In truth, now that I think on it, she might be accused by some of being calculating."

"You mean by that, sir, that for some reason it was in her best interest to take the floor with you?"

"It is possible, Miss Damion."

"But you did not think of that at the time, even though you knew my sister was waiting?"

"There scarcely seemed time to think," he told her with a sudden flare of defiance. "She took my arm and . . . "

"Ah, she is an Amazon of some sort then, I think, if she forcibly swayed you from your course."

"I think that you are mocking me," Lord Watching said, starting to rise.

"It was you who expressed a wish to make an explanation," Jennifer reminded him.

"Ah yes, it was," he muttered, sinking back against the cushions and passing one hand over his eyes. "Very well, then, I can be honest with myself, I think. The lady is no Amazon except in regard to having an extraordinarily strong will. It was weak of me not to make my excuses and leave her and it was no more than I deserved that I was not given the opportunity to speak to your sister again that evening."

Jennifer smiled her approval.

"But I will be prepared another time," Lord Watching assured her and would have gone on had not the door burst open and Amelia, carrying her mother in tow, burst into the room.

If Jennifer was dismayed, her companion was aghast. Rising, he made a bow and, picking up his hat, made other indications that he was just about to leave. But Amelia would have none of it.

"The very person I wanted to see!" she cried in an excess of delight. "Dear Lord Watching! What a pleasant evening it was! Do you not agree? Here, let me put your hat away for you. I expect you have just arrived! How pleasant that the four of us can have a little chat. Dear Jennifer! Mama, do take that chair and I will sit beside Lord Watching on the sofa. What a delightful day it is, is it not! La, Jennifer, we passed Uncle on the way and I declare he looked quite debonair! You must tell us all about his cure. His doctor must be a genius, I'm sure."

"I think, my dear, that we had best be on to the Pump Room," Lady Daphne said with all the conviction of one who is certain to be overridden.

"Nonsense!" Amelia cried. "There is no hurry to that."

"But you were in a fit of impatience to go there until we passed Lord Watching's curricle outside," her mother said with a flicker of spirit of the sort Jennifer could not help but admire.

186

"I declare one curricle looks as much like any other to me to be of no matter," Amelia replied with a glance which spoke volumes in the way of warning. "Tell us about Susan, Jennifer, do, for we saw her and Lady Tassing riding with that unfortunate gentleman . . . "

"If you mean Sir John Evans, I think you know his name well enough to speak of him directly," Jennifer replied dryly.

"Yes, my dear, as I recall not over a week ago his name was not often far from your lips," Lady Daphne declared.

"That was before . . . "

"Before you found he had no fortune?" Jennifer suggested.

"Before I found we had nothing in common, Cousin," Amelia said sharply, having the good grace to flush. "Indeed, I cannot think what you are about, letting Susan show herself with such an impostor."

"But I understood that Sir John made no secret of his financial state to you, my dear," her mother said in a sweet voice which boded no good.

Lord Watching, who had remained standing through all this, glanced from Lady Daphne to Jennifer with an expression of bewilderment common to gentlemen who are granted the opportunity to see ladies unsheath their weapons in a manner which is usually reserved for the privacy of female company.

"I declare, I do not like to hear Sir John slandered," he said in a low voice, "for although I do not understand certain things about him, I believe that he is honorable."

"Then I must fault your judgment, sir," Amelia said impetuously.

"I think there is no more to be said on the subject," Lord Watching said with a firmness Jennifer had never heard in his voice before. "I hope, Miss Damion, that I can still hope for your company in a ride about town this morning."

"Why, yes, I think you can," Jennifer said, quickly disguising the fact that it was the first time such a project had been suggested. "Since my aunt and cousin are eager to go on to the Pump Room . . . "

"La, dear! We would not keep you from your own entertainment for all the world!" Lady Daphne exclaimed. "Come, Amelia, we must be on our way."

For the first time Jennifer saw her cousin truly disconcerted. And yet she could not be subdued so quickly.

"A ride about town!" she declared. "How pleasant! It is always best to travel in an open curricle on such a pleasant day. We only have Mama's lozenged coach, of course."

She stared at Lord Watching hopefully, but when he made no attempt to extend the invitation she clearly saw herself defeated. But only for the present.

"Dear Jennifer!" she cried, embracing her cousin. "How kind Lord Watching is, to be sure. It must be very lonesome for you with Uncle and Susan off on their own affairs! Good-bye, Lord Watching! Perhaps Mama and I can expect a visit from you this afternoon when you are free from your obligations. It is just so with us in the the country. Affairs of charity do so occupy the mornings!"

And with that parting thrust, she billowed out the door in a wave of pink and white muslin.

"Do not mind her, Jennie," Lady Daphne said in a low voice, kissing her niece. "She is not used to disappointment, but I think it will do her good."

"I hope I was not rude to excess," Lord Watching said when they were gone. "You know, of course, that my suggestion that we ride together had nothing of charity about it."

"Charity to yourself, perhaps," Jennifer said with a smile. "But I will hold you to it, sir. One moment while I fetch my pelisse and bonnet."

It was indeed a brilliant morning with the sun skirting every cloud and the streets aglitter with ladies and gentlemen on foot and in their carriages. Lord Watching was so pleased with himself that at first he drove with a certain abandon which put Jennifer's teeth on edge, but after a

189

while he allowed the horses to settle to a steady gait and turned to her in a confidential manner.

"I believe I have begun to see things in a clearer light," he said. "At least I know your cousin for what she is and will behave accordingly in the future, I assure you."

"That is a great something," Jennifer said dryly.

"But something distresses me," he continued, sliding the reins into one hand while he adjusted his beaver hat, which the swaying motion of their progress had threatened to dislodge. "And that concerns Sir John Evans."

"You defended him well, sir. And, I think, with justice."

"I am not so certain of that," Lord Watching said. "Granted that I do not believe that he sought to mislead anyone in regards to his fortune, but it would seem to me there is another reason why your sister should be encouraged not to see too much of the gentleman."

"And what is that?" Jennifer said, startled.

"I think that he is fickle, Miss Damion," Lord Watching said with the air of one making a decisive judgment. "I know the word is more often applied to ladies, but you will recall, I think, that he first appeared to set his cap for your cousin, and then he turned quite easily to your sister. Why, he would not let me near her last night! And now he has taken her riding this morning! I think perhaps she should not trust his intentions."

"Why, as for that, sir," Jennifer replied, "a casual observer might think it odd that not three weeks ago you were my cousin's constant companion, and then your interest seemed to turn to me and then . . ."

"But you told me that we could be nothing but friends, Miss Damion, and as soon as you had said it I saw that it was so."

"Do not interrupt me, pray," she told him. "You seemed quite ready to pay a certain attention to my sister subsequently. You call Sir John fickle. But do you not think, on your own account, you must confess that appearances may be misleading?"

"I hope you do not think that it was simply a passing fancy which made me eager to impress your sister, Miss Damion!" Lord Watching exclaimed, letting the reins fall to the floor in his agitation. "Let me be frank with you. It burst on me all of a sudden that her goodness and her innocence were without price and that only in her presence did I see myself the man I wish to be."

"You express yourself so eloquently that I cannot but believe you," Jennifer told him in a low voice. "We can only hope that you still have a chance with her."

The curricle had come to a standstill outside a magnificent private house of which the two young people were only dimly aware until quite suddenly an elegant barouche drew in beside them and a gentleman whom Jennifer recognized as Lord Bemis descended to the street and proceeded to mount the stairs to the residence.

And then, without warning, a young woman with disheveled red hair flying appeared from the area stairs which reached below the street and began screaming. A crowd had already gathered before Jennifer saw that it was Molly.

"Oh, help me someone!" the abigail was crying. "On a simple errand, I was, and found myself assaulted! Only look at the disarray in which I have been put!"

And with that she began to tear at the bodice of her gown in such a distracted fashion that a good deal of her milk-white bosom was soon in view.

"Molly!" Jennifer cried, leaping down from the curricle.

But Molly was not to be interrupted in the midst of her histrionics, but was even now kneeling before Lord Bemis, who had descended to the street wearing a bewildered expression.

"Oh, sir, it was your Alfred!" Molly cried.

"Damn the fellow!" Lord Bemis shouted. "If he has violated you, Miss, it will be the worse for him!"

Shouts of approval rose from the crowd as Jennifer attempted to push her way through.

"Marriage is all I ask, sir!" she heard Molly cry.

"I want nothing more than that he should make an honest woman of me! La, Miss! What are you doing here!"

"Trying to save our family from scandal," Jennifer declared, making some attempt to pull the bodice of the abigail's gown together. "Come. Get in the carriage! And stop your shrieking!"

"An honest woman!" Molly cried as Jennifer pulled her toward the waiting curricle where Lord Watching sat as one thunderstruck.

"Alfred will make you that, I promise you!" Lord Bemis declared.

"Well then," Molly murmured as Jennifer helped her into the carriage, "I am well satisfied. And what will your uncle think, Miss, when he learns of this?"

"I expect he will be well enough pleased to be rid of you," Jennifer said sharply and then relented when the abigail covered her face with her hands.

"Come, you know that was very bad of you," Jennifer went on in a gentler voice as Lord Watching spurred the horses. "To trick Alfred as you did! Still, he *did* play the trickster first. And I did not mean what I said. We will miss you very much indeed. Pray, do stop crying, Molly!"

Slowly the abigail withdrew her fingers from her face, and instead of tears, Jennifer saw laughter in her eyes.

"Oh, Miss!" the girl exclaimed. "I could not help giving in to a few giggles like. Now, if your uncle can bring himself to see the funny side of it, all will be well enough, I'm sure."

Chapter Sixteen

However, it was immediately apparent on their return to Gay Street that the Duke of Jennings was in no mood to see the humor of anything. Having taken leave of a curiously distracted Lord Watching at the door, Jennifer and Molly found His Grace sprawled in his armchair, groaning loudly. Pills littered the table beside him and every bottle of medicine stood uncapped while Jack was busy bandaging the gouty foot which was propped high on a footstool in the old manner.

"Why, whatever has brought about a relapse, Uncle?" Jennifer said with genuine concern. "Has the doctor been sent for?"

Clutching his heart with one hand and his head with the other, the Duke proceeded to groan even

195

louder, which Jennifer took to be an indication that he did not care to indulge in conversation.

"Do you want me to tell him the good news about Alfred, Miss?" Molly whispered. "It might do to raise his spirits for I'm sure he'd see the humor in it."

Jennifer shook her head and listened to Jack's account of how he had tried to reason with his master as to the necessity of calling a doctor.

"But he wouldn't hear of it, Miss, and that's a fact," the manservant concluded, keeping hard at work on the bandage which was now assuming gigantic proportions.

"If Your Grace would like to hear a fine story," Molly began.

"Upstairs with you!" Jennifer hissed. "Make yourself presentable and then be off to fetch the doctor! Let's hear no more of storytelling!"

The look in her eyes was enough to subdue the abigail and she scurried off, allowing Jennifer to turn her full attention to her uncle, whose groans had reached such a pitch that she feared he might do violence to his vocal cords.

"Has he taken any laudanum, Jack?" she demanded.

"No, Miss," the valet replied, putting a finishing touch on the bandage and wiping the perspiration from his forehead with the arm of his jacket. "The fact is, he hasn't dosed himself with any-

196

thing. Just taken all the tops off bottles and the like."

For the first time since she had entered the room, it came to Jennifer's mind that all this commotion was more by way of show than anything, and this idea was fortified when she noted that her uncle was staring at her speculatively through his fingers, although his uncovered eye remained closed.

"Now, Uncle," she declared, pouring a generous measure of laudanum into a glass and adding a bit of water from the pitcher, "take this. It will calm you."

"And what if I do not wish to be calm, gel?" the Duke of Jennings demanded, giving over groaning as she pressed the glass to his lips.

"Well, do you not wish to have your pain relieved?" Jennifer demanded.

"There's only one thing I want," he assured her, "and that's to return to the country. Damme, I'll show my back to this hellhole! See if I don't, and that as soon as possible."

"Sick as you appear to be, there can be no question of traveling," Jennifer assured him firmly. "Now, drink this, do, or I will lose all patience with you."

Perhaps because he was as much surprised by hearing the threat as Jennifer was to have uttered it, the Duke obediently swallowed the medicine and made a face.

"And now," Jennifer said, sinking onto the footstool and assuming a gentler tone of voice, "perhaps you will tell me what it was that brought on this attack. I confess I had thought you quite recovered."

"It was only a remission," the Duke grumbled. "How could it have been anything else, given the state of my health? You ought not to have let me go out, indeed you should not, for see what has come of it."

"Did the attack take you before or after you met Lady Flauntington?" Jennifer asked him innocently enough.

"Do not speak of Lady Flauntington to me!" her uncle shouted, and then proceeded to groan again more loudly than before.

"You had better allow Jack to assist you to your bed, Uncle," Jennifer said in a conciliatory voice, "for it is clear that, for some reason or other, conversation will do you no good. If you will simply lie quietly, the laudanum will soon do its work."

"Damme, I would like nothing better than a sound sleep," the Duke replied as the valet helped him to his feet. "Indeed nothing would suit me better than that I should never awake. Oh, my head! My heart! My leg! I wonder that I can bear it!"

His parting words gave Jennifer some cause for concern since never before had she seen him in a mood which seemed so closely to border on despair. Indeed her uncle had such an abiding fear of death that she had never heard him mention it before, no matter how indirectly. But she had no time to puzzle over the matter before Mrs. Capstone appeared to announce Lady Daphne, who came fluttering into the room, her bonnet somewhat awry and her usually pale face quite flushed.

"Oh, my dear!" she cried, embracing Jennifer. "How is my brother? After what I have just heard I would not be surprised to learn that he has suffered a severe relapse!"

The sound of groans from the next room was all the answer she needed, apparently, for letting her pelisse slip to the floor, she drew Jennifer down onto the sofa beside her.

"Has he told you everything?" she demanded. "I came away from the Pump Room directly I heard the news. I declare, I did not even try to persuade Amelia to come with me for she would do nothing but speak of the humiliation of it."

"Of what, Aunt?" Jennifer said anxiously. "Uncle told me nothing. Whatever can have happened?"

"I would never have believed it if Lady Fulton had not sworn that she had seen it all with her very eyes, and, as you may know, she is someone to be believed. The entire room was abuzz with it. Why, it will be the talk of Bath for weeks, I declare!"

"It is not like you to be so slow in coming to the point, Aunt," Jennifer said in a fit of impatience. "What is it Lady Fulton saw?"

"She said that she would not have been surprised to see it come to fisticuffs except that my brother suddenly suffered an attack and had to be helped from the room and into his carriage."

"It would be better to proceed from the beginning rather than the end," Jennifer suggested. "You cannot mean that someone challenged Uncle to a fight."

"But that is exactly what I *do* mean, my dear!" Lady Daphne exclaimed, drawing her fan out of her reticule with shaking fingers and proceeding to wave it about with such violence that Jennifer was forced to duck her head. "I have never seen Lord Flauntington myself, but they tell me he is a giant of a man and quite fit. What your uncle would have done had he been physically accosted, I'm sure I do not know!"

"Lord Flauntington!" Jennifer cried. "But I did not know he was in Bath. Lady Tassing only said that he and his wife had separated."

"The separation was only on her part, it seems," Lady Daphine said weakly. "Oh my, how close it is in here. Open a window, do, my dear!"

"Yes, Aunt," Jennifer replied, rising. "But must I guess what has happened?"

"It would be much simpler for me if you did,"

Lady Daphne declared, "for I find I do not convey scandal well."

"Was this the way of it then?" Jennifer asked, taking her seat again, this time at a safer distance from the maneuvers of the fan. "Uncle went to the Pump Room to meet Lady Flauntington, I know, although I believe Lady Tassing would have prevented him from doing so had she been given an opportunity."

"What he could have been thinking about I do not know!" Lady Daphne cried.

"When he met the lady yesterday, I believe he found her a fascinating source of gossip," Jennifer replied. "Thanks to Molly, gossip has become his passion of late. But I am certain there was no more to this morning's meeting than his desire to hear more."

"What his intent might have been is quite beside the point now," her aunt assured her, "for Lady Fulton assures me that when Lord Flauntington burst into the room and saw the two of them taking the waters together and talking in quite an intimate manner, he was like an enraged beast. Yes, those were her very words! I am only glad that Amelia delayed our arrival by insisting in a long conversation with the Marquess of Newly with the consequence that when we reached the Pump Room it was all over. Why, if I had been there, I am sure I would have fainted, for you know, my dear, how I detest violence in any form."

"Yes, yes," Jennifer said impatiently. "But was that the extent of it? I mean to say, did Lord Flauntington interrupt the two and threaten to strike Uncle? Not that that is not bad enough but . . ."

"Oh, there was even worse," her aunt assured her, "for Lady Fulton tells me that Lord Flauntington declared that he had been cuckolded and . . ."

"Cuckolded! By Uncle? But that is too absurd!"

"I declare Lord Flauntington seems to have found nothing absurd in the idea. Lady Fulton tells me that he was even more plainspoken than that and accused his wife of being an unfaithful jade."

"This is very bad," Jennifer said in a low voice.

"But there is more!" her aunt exclaimed, losing her grip on the fan with the result that it flew across the room and struck a small vase on the mantelpiece.

"Yes," Lady Daphne continued over the sound of shattering glass. "Lord Flauntington said that he intended to go to the law."

"The law!"

"He spoke of alienation of affection, I believe," her aunt told her, "and when your uncle protested the other gentleman raised his fists and Lady Flauntington screamed and there was a general turmoil."

"In the midst of which Uncle had his attack?"

"That was just the way of it, my dear."

"Well, that at least was clever of him," Jennifer declared.

"You mean that he was only pretending to be ill?"

"We will not know for certain until the effects of the laudanum I gave him wear off," Jennifer said thoughtfully. "But I think he was making a show of too many pains. Indeed, he had taken every trick from the bag and tried them all on at once. Do not think I mean to be disrespectful but . . ."

"I know my brother as well as you," Lady Daphne assured her, "and now that I think on it the attack *was* most convenient. I declare, that is one worry off my mind, at least. If he is not truly ill . . . Amelia! What are you doing here?"

"We will be forced to leave Bath!" her daughter cried, slamming the door behind her. "And as for London, we will never be able to show our faces there again! We might have overcome one scandal, but two in the same day is too much! It is all your fault, Jennifer. Indeed, I think you allowed everything to happen as it did for no better reason than to blight my chances, for how I can seriously be considered on the marriage mart now, I do not know!"

Jennifer uttered no disclaimer, being too startled by Amelia's Medea-like appearance to do so.

Never before had she seen even so much as a bit of lace out of place in her cousin's costume, but now Amelia appeared quite disheveled, her bonnet hanging from her neck by its ribbons and the hem of her blue silk gown covered with mud as though she had made her way through a considerable puddle.

"You must not blame your uncle, child," Lady Daphne declared, "for Jennifer assures me that he met with Lady Flauntington in all innocence and . . ."

"No one will ever believe that!" Amelia exclaimed. "Particularly since he saw fit to play the rake on the same day that Molly allowed herself to be molested by one of Lord Bemis's footmen!"

"Molly molested!" Lady Daphne exclaimed. "Why, I would not have thought it possible!"

"No more was it," Jennifer assured her. "It was all a trick to force the fellow to marry her. But surely, Amelia, the antics of our abigail cannot be public knowledge!"

"How do you think I came to hear of it otherwise?" Amelia demanded, tearing the ribbons of her bonnet apart and flinging it to the floor in a fit of passion. "From what I heard, it was far from being a trick. Why, they say that she was struggling with the footman in the street and that the upper part of her gown had been ripped from her shoulders. They say it took five men to force the

fellow away from her and that she cried that she
had been . . . "

"Amelia!" Lady Daphne exclaimed. "There is
no use in repeating every word you heard, particularly since Jennifer assures us that it is not true."

"The report has been much exaggerated, Aunt,"
Jennifer assured her.

"And what does it matter whether it has or
hasn't?" Amelia demanded, still in a fury. "Between Molly and my uncle we will be the laugh-
ingstock of Bath."

"It does not follow that whoever chooses to
laugh at them will laugh at you," Jennifer said in
icy tones. "I think you take these matters too personally by far, Cousin. Much as you like to imagine you are the object of some interest, I fancy that
very few people are aware of the connection between our families, and those that do could care
less."

"Well, as for that . . . " Amelia began, her face
turning a fiery red.

"Hold your tongue, Daughter, do!" Lady Daphne
declared with an unusual show of asperity. "You
might have grace enough to show some sympathy
for your uncle, for I am sure he meant no harm. Yet
he may have a lawsuit on his hands."

"That should be of little importance to someone
with his wealth," Amelia retorted. "But as for me,
I must marry well. It is a hard burden to bear and

I would not have you make little of it, Mama. I must think to myself."

"I have not seen you think of anyone else from the moment you were able to toddle about the floor," her mother replied sharply. "Your father left us with a sufficiency, as you well know. If you hope to 'marry well,' as you put it, that is your own decision."

"Mama!" Amelia wailed. "You have never spoken to me like this before! I will not have it!"

"You should have had a good deal more of it besides," Lady Daphne assured her. "I have been far too indulgent with you, as I see now to my sorrow. You are a bore, Amelia, with your constant talk of I—I—I, and I declare that Jennifer must be as tired of listening to you as I am."

Amelia tried to speak, but no words came. And in silence which followed, all three ladies heard the sound of running feet upon the stairs.

"It must be Molly and the doctor," Jennifer said in a low voice, hurrying to the door.

But it was Susan and Lady Tassing who made their appearance, both of them flushed and panting.

"Oh, it is terrible! Terrible!" Susan cried, casting herself into Jennifer's arms.

"Yes, something must be done to prevent it!" Lady Tassing exclaimed, sinking onto the sofa beside Lady Daphne.

"The damage is done, I fear," Jennifer told

them. "And, indeed, it may not be as bad as you think, for perhaps Lord Flauntington will desist on reflection, and as for Molly . . . "

"I do not know what you are talking about, Jennie!" Susan said in a shrill voice. "Lord Flauntington and Molly have nothing to do with this."

"We bring news of Sir John Evans and Lord Watching!" Lady Tassing declared, closing her eyes and taking deep gulps of air. "Oh, dear, I believe that I may swoon!"

"Another scandal!" Amelia cried.

"Worse than a scandal," Susan assured her, continuing to cling to Jennifer. "Oh, Jennie, Jennie, whatever will we do? Lord Watching has challenged Sir John to a duel."

Chapter Seventeen

For a while chaos reigned in the little sitting room as Jennifer hurried to fetch a vinaigrette for Lady Tassing while Susan gave way to hysteria and Amelia demanded explanations in a loud voice. In the midst of this confusion Molly arrived with the doctor whereupon Lady Tassing, hearing of the Duke's attack for the first time, threw the vinaigrette to the floor and demanded access to his chamber.

In the midst of all this, Jennifer managed a quiet word with the physician and, with a show of calm she was far from feeling, explained that she had dosed her uncle with laudanum and that an examination must wait until the following day.

When the doctor had taken his leave, not without first casting a puzzled look around the room, Jennifer turned her attention to Lady Tassing, preventing her from forcing her way into the Duke of Jennings's chamber by giving the same excuse she had given the physician. It was only when all this had been accomplished that she became aware of the violent quarrel taking place between Amelia and Molly, the former hurling accusations left and right, while the abigail defended herself stoutly.

"Let us have quiet!" Jennifer demanded. "Molly, leave the room, if you please!"

"And have *her* call me names behind my back?" the abigail declared. "I'll leave if *she* will, but not before!"

This speech was delivered with one finger pointed at Amelia, who turned on Jennifer in a rage.

"Will you let one of your menials speak to me like this?" she demanded.

"I'm not to be spoken of as a menial!" Molly declared. "Nor as a servant, either, for I'll be giving my notice soon enough."

"If I were you, Cousin," Amelia cried, "I would be giving her her notice now!"

"Does no one care about Lord Watching and Sir John?" Susan demanded tearfully.

"If what you say is true," Amelia retorted, "they are both greater fools than I thought. I have no sympathy with anyone who duels. Why, Mr. Nash made it quite clear that there were to be no duels in Bath and I expect . . . "

"It does not matter to us a whit what you expect, my dear," her mother told her. "Leave us, pray!"

Snatching up her bonnet, Amelia fled the room with Molly, apparently intent on obtaining some apology, close on her heels. For a moment they could be heard quarreling in the hallway and then there was quiet.

"Now," Jennifer said wearily, "will you kindly make an explanation, Susan?"

"Why, it happened so suddenly that I do not know what to think even now," her sister said, choking back a sob. "Sir John had reined his horses near the watering trough in the center of town and was laughing at something I had said when Lord Watching drove up in his curricle and halted."

"He stared at us in such a curious manner," Lady Tassing interrupted, "that I knew at once that something was wrong."

"Sir John greeted him in a friendly enough fashion," Susan went on, dabbing at her eyes with a handkerchief. "And so did I."

"I think you may have seemed a little cool, my dear," Lady Tassing suggested, "for if you recall correctly, you did not smile and turned your back on him almost at once."

"Well, that was simply pique and meant nothing," Susan protested. "After all, he had left me unaccompanied to go off with Amelia the evening before. Surely he had no right to expect me to behave as though there was nothing to forgive!"

"That may be fair enough," Lady Tassing told her, "but I was facing him and I saw his expression change the instant you snubbed him. And then, of course, you did drop your reticule and, although it was only by chance, I know that Sir John happened to touch your hand when he returned it to you . . . "

"I declare I felt nothing!" Susan cried.

"But you did murmur your thanks while his face was still quite close to yours. It may have appeared to Lord Watching that there was a certain amount of flirtation being engaged in."

"And what of it if there was!" Susan declared, emerging red-eyed from the cover of her handkerchief.

"Can you not go on with the story?" Jennifer said impatiently.

"Yes. Give us the broad outline first and let the details wait until later," Lady Daphne urged.

"Well, I declare, there is little enough left to tell," Lady Tassing assured her. "Lord Watching drew off his gloves, ever so slowly, and then he got down from his curricle and came to stand beside us."

"And then he asked Sir John what his intentions were," Susan added, beginning to weep again as though the scene was too much for her to remember.

"And what reply did Sir John make?" Jennifer demanded.

"Why, he simply said he did not know what Lord Watching meant," Lady Tassing said. "He was very cool, I must say, but watching the other gentleman every moment."

"That was when Lord Watching called him a bounder!" Susan cried. "I declare, I could not believe my ears and I think Sir John could not either, for he did not move or speak until Lord Watching flung one of his gloves in his face."

"And then?" Jennifer said in a low voice.

"Why, then Lord Watching called him out!" Susan cried.

"And Sir John bowed his head and thought for a moment," Lady Tassing added. "And then he said he would send his second to Lord Watching to make the necessary arrangements. Oh dear, all this and your uncle ill again! I wish none of us had ever set foot in this detestable town!"

"And so do I," Jennifer murmured. "However, the damage has been done, and we must make what effort we can to undo it."

"I do not think what you can mean, my dear," Lady Daphne said in a gentle voice. "I know how concerned you must be, but this is gentlemen's business and they will brook no interference."

"That is the usual way of looking at things, I

know," Jennifer said thoughtfully. "But since they have taken it on themselves to behave like fools—and I do agree with Amelia in that—they must be interfered with, I think."

"But what do you intend to do?" Susan cried.

"I think that I will go to see Sir John at his lodgings," Jennifer replied briskly.

"But you cannot go alone!" Lady Tassing exclaimed. "If you were seen, think of the scandal!"

"One more touch of scandal will not do us any harm, I think," Jennifer said dryly.

"Only take me with you, my dear," Lady Daphne implored her.

Jennifer shook her head.

"I think that I must speak to the gentleman alone," she said in a low voice.

"But what do you mean by saying one more touch of scandal will not harm you?" Lady Tassing demanded.

"I think I must leave my aunt to explain all that to you and Susan," Jennifer told her. "The sooner I am on my way the better. Perhaps I will return with better news than we have heard this day."

Chapter Eighteen

Because of the many outings the young people had taken together in happier times, there was no need for Jennifer to ask directions to the modest lodging house on Ram Street where Sir John Evans had taken rooms. Since it was only a short distance away, there was no need for her to take her uncle's carriage and, indeed, she needed the walk to give her an opportunity to think, for there was much about what had happened to puzzle her.

The foremost question in her mind was as to why Lord Watching had chosen to insult Sir John and then challenge him to a duel. Of all the gentlemen Jennifer knew, she thought Watching was the least likely to take such a step. And yet, as she walked down the crowded street, a slim graceful figure in her sprigged muslin gown, it came to her that if she could put herself in his place for a few minutes of thought, at least, she might be able to understand.

First and foremost, she must assume that Lord Watching sincerely cared for Susan and that, no doubt, it was the first time his heart had been truly touched. He had thought himself in love before, first with Amelia, who had coolly jilted him, and then with herself. She remembered how she had cautioned him not to let his emotions too easily be touched. Indeed, she had played the schoolmistress with him after having deliberately led him on.

And so she must think of him as someone who had been manipulated twice. And she had been fool enough to think that because he was, in many ways, naive, he would not be hurt too badly. And perhaps, because he had not really cared for either her or Amelia, he had not been. But the fear of further manipulation must have been there, ever deepening. After all, this was the gentleman who had told her on the first occasion of their meeting that he had no friends and that his sudden advancement in life had made him every man and woman's prey.

Then he had seen Susan for what she truly was, gay and innocent and completely without guile. And he had formed a real attachment which had no sooner budded when he had been forced to place himself in a bad light, thanks to Amelia's importuning. How frustrated he must have been. And yet, no doubt, he had hoped that Susan would listen to his excuse and understand. But when he had come to offer his apologies, she had been off on the arm of another gentleman, and that no less than the person who had distracted Amelia's attention away from him not long before. Jennifer remembered how, in the carriage that morning, he had told her that he feared that Sir John was not as honorable as he had thought him.

And then she remembered the look in Lord Watching's eyes when he had set her and Molly down in front of the house on Gay Street. It had been the look of a man engrossed in his own thoughts. And what those thoughts might have been, she could only guess.

The final thrust to his pride, not to mention his heart, must have come when he had seen Susan and Sir John together in the curricle. How cold Susan must have seemed, a different person entirely than he had imagined her. And then when Sir John had bent to pick up the reticule which had fallen to the carriage floor . . . It must have appeared to Lord Watching that Susan was as fickle as any other woman he had met, or as uncaring, and that she was being lured into a flirtation. Under such circumstances was it not certain that his anger and disappointment would have turned to a desire for revenge and that Sir John must be its object?

Jennifer had been so lost in thought that she had missed the turning to Ram Street, but she roused herself as a butcher's boy ran full tilt into her and at once corrected her mistake. Within two minutes she was lowering a tarnished knocker in the shape of a lion's head against its equally tarnished brass plate.

The landlady, if that was who she was, answered the door by peeking around it in a suspicious manner, and it was only when Jennifer assured her that she had pressing business with Sir John Evans that the lady consented to see if he was in. Left waiting on the doorstep, Jennifer felt the first tinge of humiliation and had all that she could do to keep from looking around to see if she was being observed. Shoulders stiff, she reminded herself that the reason for her coming here was so urgent that it would not do for her to care what others thought.

When the landlady returned and grudgingly admitted her, it was all too easy to guess what was going through her mind. As she directed Jennifer to go up the stairs to the first landing and turn right, the girl imagined that the miserable old woman was thinking that she was some impetuous young thing who, having been jilted perhaps, had come to see Sir John to seek reassurance. Her cheeks burning, but with head held high, Jennifer mounted the narrow stairs and rapped at the door to which she had been directed.

Sir John opened it in an instant, a look of amazement on his face.

"Miss Damion!" he exclaimed. "What on earth are you doing here? When the landlady told me that someone was asking for me, I did not imagine it might be you! Come in at once! Or perhaps it might be best if I had my curricle brought around so that this interview might take place in public. Never for an instance would I be the cause of any slur being brought to your name."

"My family's name has been brought into question often enough today, directly or indirectly, not to make that of any particular importance," Jennifer assured him dryly.

The uncharacteristic nature of Sir John's welcome was enough to assure her that he was more unnerved than she had ever seen him, and somehow this was enough to make her even more nervous than she had been before. Jennifer steadied herself by looking about the small sitting room, which was brightened only by the display of a few personal odds and ends such as two fine watercolors on the wall and a vase of daffodils.

"You have made yourself quite comfortable, I see," she murmured, taking one of the wing chairs which were set by the bay window.

"Yes, yes," Sir John said impatiently, sitting

opposite her, his eyes hooded now. "But you must tell me what has brought you here."

"I think that you might be able to guess the reason, sir," Jennifer said firmly. "My sister and Lady Tassing only just now brought me the news. You can imagine how put about they were."

"Ah, yes. Lord Watching's challenge," he replied slowly. "An unfortunate affair, that, but one which I have no choice but to honor. But just now you spoke of scandal. Surely you must realize that I have no intention of letting this affect your family's name."

"I referred to an incident which concerns my uncle and to another involving my abigail," Jennifer told him. "Neither of which is of any importance when compared to this madness on your part, sir."

"You speak very directly," Sir John replied. "But then that is your way, as I should know by now."

"Then let me add something which has just occurred to me," Jennifer declared. "It was not what brought me here, but may I add to all the obvious arguments against the course you and Lord Watching have set the fact that it will soon be all over Bath that you have quarreled over my sister. A duel will not reflect well on her, I think, and she is quite unworthy of such treatment on the part of either of you two gentlemen."

"To that I most sincerely agree," he told her, inclining his head in such a way as to place his in the shadows. "It was to that end that I urged your sister and Lady Tassing to keep the matter quiet, for although Watching chose to challenge me in the very center of town, it happened so quickly and with no voices raised that I think it may have passed unattended."

"You are more optimistic than I, sir," Jennifer assured him. "A brief stay is all that is required in Bath to assure one that nothing that happens goes unobserved."

"Including your visit here," he suggested.

"Whether or not I care to risk my reputation is my concern," Jennifer assured him. "Let us not stray from the subject. Even if the exchange between you and Lord Watching was not noticed, you should know that Amelia and her mother were with me when Susan and Lady Tassing returned with their news. And although my aunt can be trusted to keep quiet about the affair, I doubt that the same can be said for my cousin."

"I expect you are right, Miss Damion," Sir John said thoughtfully. "It was indeed unfortunate that she chanced to be on hand to hear the news. "Is it not possible for you to speak to your cousin and . . ."

"Amelia is in a bearish mood for her own reasons," Jennifer assured him, "and will pay little attention to anything I say at this point, I think. No, if you are truly concerned with my sister's reputation, you can do no better than to call the duel off. It can be put about that it was all a joke. People will believe that, for everyone knows that you and Lord Watching have been friends."

"It was his decision that we be friends no longer," Sir John reminded her. "He is the one who can withdraw the challenge if he pleases. As a man of honor I can do nothing more than to follow his lead in the matter."

"I cannot think that honor has anything to do with such foolishness!" Jennifer exclaimed, rising and turning away from him to stare blindly out the windows. "You are the older and presumably the wiser. How can you sit and countenance what amounts to murder?"

He came to stand behind her and, for a moment, Jennifer thought that his hands hovered over her shoulders as though he would turn her to face him.

"There will be no murder," he said in a low voice. "You must believe me when I assure you that no blood will be shed."

"What can you do to ensure that except to fire your pistol over Lord Watching's head?" Jennifer demanded, turning. "And even if you do, how can you be certain that he will do the same? His pride has been hurt. Even worse, he has seen a lady he has some considerable affection for turn her back on him because of you."

"I know that is how it must seem to him," Sir

John replied. "And I am sorry for it. I did not intend . . . "

"You did not intend!" Jennifer said angrily. "Perhaps not that it would come to this, but you could not keep from meddling, could you? Oh, no doubt your intentions were for the best. You meant to comfort Susan by paying her attention when she had been slighted. Perhaps you even meant to make Lord Watching jealous. Well, you have succeeded, sir, and I hope you are happy with the results!"

"I am only happy about one thing," he assured her as she pushed past him. "And that is that Watching has set his affections on someone so deserving as your sister. When all this is over . . . "

"When all this is over, you may well be dead, sir!" Jennifer cried, her hand on the knob of the door.

"Before you leave, you must tell me one thing, Miss Damion," Sir John said, making no attempt to follow her. "And that is why you chose to come to me instead of going to Lord Watching. After all, as I have said, he is the one who can withdraw the challenge."

"I thought that I could reason best with you," Jennifer replied, glad that her back was to him so that he could not see her flush. "I had hoped to find you reasonable, but I had forgotten such manly virtues as your so-called honor!"

There was nothing more to say, or, if there was,

she did not dare remain to say it. Slamming the door shut behind her, she hurried down the stairs, pressing her fingers against her eyes to keep back the tears.

Chapter Nineteen

By the time Jennifer reached the house on Gay Street, she had regained her self-possession at least to the degree that anger was the only emotion she had allowed to surface. If two grown men were prepared to risk their lives, she told herself as she hurried up the stairs, clearly there was nothing she could do to stop them. Whatever catastrophe befell, they would have invited it.

And yet when she saw her sister's white face, the anxiety which had sent her to Sir John Evans returned to haunt her.

"What did he say, Jennie?" Susan demanded, starting up from her chair. "Is the duel to be called off?"

"He says that there is nothing he can do to prevent it," Jennifer told her wearily. "It seems the encounter will only be prevented if Lord Watching can be prevailed upon to withdraw the challenge."

Susan gave a little cry and Lady Tassing hurried across the room to put her arms about the girl.

"Do not despair," Jennifer told her sister. "I have not had time to give the matter proper thought, but I believe that were I to use the right arguments I might be able to convince Lord Watching to do whatever is necessary to put an end to this folly."

"The fact is that I thought the same thing," Susan said in a low voice. "Indeed, directly after you left us, I sent him a message begging him to reconsider. I even went so far as to suggest that he allow me to talk to him, for I cannot bear to have him think . . . "

"Perhaps I should have prevented her from sending the note," Lady Tassing interrupted, "but she wrote it while I was busy composing a letter of my own to Lord Flauntington."

Jennifer stared at the older woman, puzzled.

"It occurred to me that if he was made aware of some precise details concerning his wife's behavior since she arrived in Bath, he might think twice before taking your uncle to the law," Lady Tassing explained. "And Molly was helpful in supplying some details of which I was not aware. Whatever else you may say about the gel, she is uncommonly obliging when it comes to backstairs gossip."

"That was an unscrupulous thing for you to do," Jennifer said smiling, her spirits lightened for an instant. "But as for your note, Susan. It may have been indelicate of you, but I think neither of us are prepared to follow the conventions at the moment. Come. Tell me! What reply did he make? Or, as seems likely from the look of you, has no response been made yet?"

"No, nor will there be," Susan said, tears trickling down her cheeks.

"But I do not understand."

"It seems that Lord Watching is determined not to be swayed in his intentions," Lady Tassing told her, "for your sister's message was returned with the seal unbroken."

"But surely Lord Watching cannot be so indifferent as to refuse a word from you, Susan!" Jennifer cried.

"It seems he gave his valet a blanket order not to receive any communication of whatever sort," her sister replied, sobbing. "He will not even know I tried to contact him until it is too late, I fear."

Instantly Jennifer's rage returned.

"What a fool all gentlemen are!" she stormed. "I declare I have no patience with them! But come, Susan. Do not cry so. Sir John assured me that no blood will be shed, although how he can be sure of such a thing I do not know."

"We must stop them!" Susan cried.

"But how can that be?" Jennifer demanded. "Still if we put our minds to it, perhaps . . . ”

She broke off as Molly tumbled into the room, her red curls flying.

"Oh, Miss, you cannot imagine!" she exclaimed.

"Surely nothing else can have gone wrong," Lady Tassing declared.

"Why, there is no wrong about this, my lady," Molly said breathlessly. "I was just now up in my chamber when I happened to glance out the window just in time to see Lord Bemis's coach draw up. And you cannot fancy who is with him! Hark, I think I hear them on the stairs this minute! La, I'm that excited I can scarcely breathe!"

Moments later Lord Bemis was ushered into the presence of four distracted ladies, a look of grim determination on his broad face. Behind him came a tall, strong-shouldered fellow dressed in blue livery.

"Oh, Alfred!" Molly cried. "Fancy your coming here!"

From the expression on the footman's face, it was clear he had not come voluntarily, although this did not seem to bother Molly, who appeared to be in a perfect ecstasy of pleasure. Only by applying strong pressure to the abigail's arm did

Jennifer prevent her from flinging herself at the unwilling object of her affection.

"Now, as to whether or not the charges brought against this young cub are true, I make no judgment," Lord Bemis announced without ado. "But begging your pardons, ladies, I thought it best to have the matter settled straightaway."

"And quite proper, too, sir!" Molly declared.

"I am pleased it meets with your approval, Miss," Lord Bemis replied with a certain heavy irony which Molly chose to ignore. "It happens that Alfred has something to say to you."

Glaring at the carpet as though it were a mortal enemy, Alfred cleared his throat but seemed incapable of speech, although his mouth opened once or twice as though he sought to make the effort.

"Very well," Lord Bemis said firmly. "I will be your spokesman if I must. Mind, you brought this on yourself! I have been warning you for years! But that's of no great matter. The fact is, Miss," he went on, turning to Molly who was having all she could do to keep from jumping up and down in her delight, "Alfred wishes to make an offer. Isn't that right, you young whelp? Eh?"

With what appeared to be a considerable effort, the footman managed to incline his head.

"Never thought I'd see the day you wouldn't have a word to say for yourself," Lord Bemis reflected. "But never mind. The sooner this is over

228

the better. You're offering this gel your hand, ain't you?"

Alfred nodded more feebly than before.

"Your hand in marriage, sir?"

Alfred could be heard to groan, but once again his head bent.

"In solemn wedlock, sir?"

Jennifer reflected that his lordship was taking a certain grim pleasure in the proceedings and might be encouraged to draw them out, despite his protests to the contrary. And although this performance might have amused her at another time, she thought she could not bear to have it distract her for a minute more than was necessary. And yet, she reminded herself, there was Molly's future to think of.

"Consider well before you answer," she said to the abigail in a low voice. "You know what manner of man he is."

"And I know even better the manner of man he will be when I am his wife, Miss," Molly hissed in reply.

Then, with a certain dignity, she took two steps forward until she was standing exactly in front of Alfred, who was still glaring at the carpet.

"I'm pleased to accept your offer, sir," she said in a low voice.

At long last Alfred raised his eyes and for a moment the two stood staring silently at one another.

Jennifer could not see Molly's face, but Alfred's bore a bewildered expression, as though he could not believe this was happening to him. And then, quite suddenly, he took a deep breath, as a runner might do when the race was over, and murmured something which caused Molly to stand on tiptoe and kiss his cheek.

"Well, then, that's done," Lord Bemis said in a self-satisfied voice. "Perhaps you young ladies will be good enough to tell your uncle I'm sorry to have robbed him of a servant. The ceremony will take place without delay, of course. No need to worry his head about arrangements."

"On the contrary," Jennifer told him. "Molly will want a proper country wedding with her mother in attendance."

Lord Bemis shrugged his shoulders.

"I will leave it in your hands then, Miss Damion," he said, making his ponderous way to the door. "Come along, Alfred, there's a good chap. Time enough for billing and cooing later."

"Why, he's a proper old muckworm!" Molly declared as soon as they were alone and she had been properly kissed by Jennifer, Susan, and Lady Tassing in turn. "But then I'll put a bit of backbone into Alfred once we're married. 'There's a good chap' indeed! But there now! That's for the future and it's the present you ladies want to be dealing with."

"Oh, Molly!" Susan cried. "We *will* be sorry to lose you!"

"And that you should," the abigail replied pertly. "I take it from the look of your eyes, Miss, that the duel's not to be prevented."

Susan answered her by bursting into tears.

"You know I'm not one to be putting myself forward, Miss," Molly continued, turning to Jennifer, "but it came to me earlier on that if you could not make the gentlemen see reason now, you might want to be on hand on the day itself."

"But that is quite impossible!" Jennifer exclaimed. "Even if we knew the time and place . . ."

"I know it's not the usual thing for ladies to put in an appearance at suchlike affairs," Molly told her, "but if it was me, I wouldn't be put off so easily."

"I think you go too far, gel," Lady Tassing began, clearly appalled.

"And I think there is some wisdom in what she is saying," Jennifer said in a low voice. "At any rate, anything is better than doing nothing."

"Oh, yes, Jennie!" Susan cried.

"Then if that's the way of it," Molly said with a broad smile, "I'll take it on myself to discover the time and place."

"But how can you do that, pray?" Jennifer demanded.

"Ask me no questions and I'll tell no lies," Molly replied with a broad wink. "I'd think by now you'd know, Miss, that there's no secrets to be kept in servants' halls."

And with that she hurried out of the room, leaving some hope behind her.

Chapter Twenty

Molly was as good as her word, and the dawn of the next day found Jennifer together with Susan and a reluctant Lady Tassing standing, well cloaked against the morning dew and shielded from view by the drooping branches of a willow tree, on the edge of a meadow two miles to the north of Bath.

The gentlemen and their seconds had arrived before them on horseback and now, as the rising sun made a golden portrait of the scene, Sir John stood leaning against a stone wall, as much at ease in his whipcord jacket, buckskins, and top boots as though he were simply making pause in an early canter, while Lord Watching stood a hundred yards away, his shoulders stiff, watching the seconds pace off a course.

"At least they have had the good sense to make their valets their attendants," Lady Tassing whispered. "It is the best way to keep the matter from becoming common knowledge."

"When I consider the apparent ease with which Molly's Alfred gained the information we wanted, I do not think they will have succeeded as well as they suppose," Jennifer replied in a low voice.

"Oh, dear," Susan murmured. "They will be so angry when they discover that we are here. And yet we had no choice but to come, had we, Jennie? I do not know why we do not make our presence known directly before they can proceed any further."

"Sir John assured me that no blood would be shed," Jennifer replied grimly, "and I am determined to let him make good his word. But if he has done nothing to keep this duel from occurring before they take their places, we will be forced to intervene."

"I declare I never should have let you come," Lady Tassing moaned, "for I have never heard of ladies presuming in such a manner."

"There must always be a first time for everything," Jennifer assured her. "Indeed, I refuse to take this barbarous ritual for anything more than

234

that. Let anyone dare to speak to me of this being a field of honor and I will . . . "

"But what are they doing now?" Susan exclaimed in some agitation.

"I know no more of the proceedings than you do," Jennifer reminded her. "But it appears that Sir John's manservant is taking a case to Lord Watching as though he wanted him to examine something."

"It is the pistols, no doubt," Lady Tassing whispered in a distracted manner. "When I was a gel dueling was quite common, of course, and I know something of it. I believe that the gentleman who is challenged has the right to choose the weapons, if he cares to."

"In that event the pistols will be Sir John's," Jennifer said. "See. His valet is raising the cover of the case and Lord Watching is looking inside."

"Oh, dear, it *is* a pistol!" Susan cried. "He is lifting it out of the case. We must stop them now!"

"Wait!" Jennifer said, taking her sister's arm. "Something strange is happening! Note how closely Lord Watching is examining the weapon. And now he is making some exclamation!"

"Why, he has thrown the thing to the ground!" Lady Tassing observed. "Whatever can be wrong?"

"And now he is pressing his hands against his face!" Susan cried. "Has he lost his courage, do you think. Oh, dear! Oh, dear! I cannot bear to think that he is about to humiliate himself. And all because of my foolish pride! We must make our presence known at once, before Sir John sees what he has done! No, do not try to hold me, Jennie!"

And tearing herself away from her sister, she began to run across the meadow, her blue cloak billowing behind her. She cried Lord Watching's name and he, raising his face from his hands, stared at her for a moment in bewilderment and then hastened toward her.

In a moment Jennifer and Lady Tassing had joined them while Sir John approached from the opposite direction and the two valets retired discreetly.

"It is my fault that you have been put in this terrible position!" Susan was crying. "And I am glad that you could not face the prospect of risking your life!"

Lord Watching's face was pinched and pale.

"I would not have you think that I could not go through with it, Miss Damion," he said in a shaken manner. "I mean by that that had I not just made a startling discovery as to the true identity of my opponent, that pistol would even now be in my hand."

"I do not understand you!" Susan cried. "What is this talk of identity?"

Lord Watching bent and picked up the pistol from the grass and they saw that it was a magnificent weapon with a long, well-polished barrel and a glistening ivory handle embossed with a gold crest.

"You meant me to see this, sir," Lord Watching said in a low voice, extending the pistol balanced in the palm of his hand to Sir John. "And now you might care to tell me why you choose such an indirect manner to let me know that you are the true Earl of Watching. For you are my uncle, sir, are you not? There is no other way this weapon could have come into your possession."

"But your uncle died in the Spanish campaign!" Jennifer cried. "You told me so yourself."

"I think this gentleman must provide us with the answers," Lord Watching said with dignity.

All eyes turned to Sir John. He had taken the pistol and was holding it carelessly at his side. But despite the ease of his bearing, his face was grim, as though some strong emotion had cast it into stone, and his eyes were hooded in the way Jennifer had come to dread.

"It is true that I am your uncle, sir," he said evenly, "and I must begin by begging you to forgive me for not telling you sooner."

"But why would you play such a cruel trick on Lord Watching?" Susan cried.

"You must call me that no longer, Miss Damion," the young gentleman beside her said gently. "I am Sir Matthew Fuller and I declare, no matter

237

what revelations my uncle may make, I am glad enough to be myself again."

"It is a great relief to me that you should feel that way," his uncle told him, "for I have had cause of late to feel guilty enough without bearing the burden of your disappointment to find me alive. Had you been the sort I feared I might find you to be when I returned to England, you would not have thrown this pistol to the ground just now. Many a man in your position would have used it against me and been free to keep the title with no one the wiser."

"You have a dark mind, sir!" Jennifer exclaimed.

"Perhaps not as dark as circumstances might make it appear," the gentleman whom she must now think of as the Earl of Watching told her, his eyes intent on hers. "Although I had not thought to find you here, I am glad enough that you should hear the explanation on the first instance of its being given."

"Whatever the explanation is, it cannot satisfy," Jennifer replied. "Too much harm has come of it."

"Why, as to that," he told her, "Matthew has been given the opportunity to know for certain that he is satisfied with his station in life. Add to that the fact that he has engaged the affections of a young lady to whom it makes no difference whether he is Earl or simple Baronet."

"What he says is true enough, Jennie," Susan said, flushing. "Do not be too hard, pray."

"Your sister must make her own decision when she hears my story," Lord Watching said evenly. "As must you, Matthew. I believe I may call you that, even though I may seem to you at present to be no real friend."

"It was my foolishness and not yours which brought us here," Sir Matthew replied. "I, for one, am willing to suspend judgment until we hear your story."

"It is a simple enough one in some ways," his uncle replied. "Two months ago, in Spain, I received a scalp wound of a serious enough nature to make my return to England necessary. However, no sooner had I arrived and gone to my solicitor when I discovered that word had preceded me of my death. Such errors occur more often than the general public knows in such troubled times."

"But surely your solicitor could have set the mistake straight in a few hours," Sir Matthew replied. "I was in London then, as he well knew, and a message could have been sent to me at once."

"I will make no excuses as to the possibility that the shock my wound had caused the system may have affected my judgment," his uncle replied, and Jennifer noted that his face had gone quite

239

white. "Although I think now that there was that possibility. You must try to understand my pattern of thought. It occurred to me, you see, that I had been presented with an opportunity rarely given to anyone who possesses substantial property. And that was the opportunity to observe precisely how my own heir would respond to the responsibilities which would one day truly come to him."

He paused. No one uttered a word. If words can be said to be hung on, so were his at this moment.

"I thought of it thus," he continued. "If I should find you competent, I would be well satisfied. If I should find you a spendthrift and a bounder, I would be able to change my will. And if, as I think now, I should find you willing but unprepared to assume the burdens of a great estate, I could subsequently keep you by my side and train you to the task."

"But you speak as though you were a great age, sir, and that is not the case," Sir Matthew exclaimed. "Did it not occur to you that since you had safely returned from Spain, you might marry and provide your own heir?"

Again the dark eyes returned to Jennifer. "You remember perhaps what I told you about the misery of my parents' marriage, Miss Damion," he said in a low voice, as though they were alone together. "That, at least, is true enough. No," he continued, turning to his nephew, "I did not think to marry."

"And so you followed me to Bath to observe my character?" Sir Matthew said in a low voice. "I think that I can understand. And if you took the bother of communicating with your estate agent you must know that my visit to the country was abortive."

"I communicated with no one," his uncle told him, "only my solicitor, and he was sworn to silence. But I presumed that since you did not remain in the country, you did not find management of that sort congenial."

"It was all a mystery to me," his nephew told him. "I saw at once that I could never take your place there. You must believe that no amount of training would suit me for the task. I was happy enough in my former life and would like to return to it."

"But will you leave all that has passed to that!" Jennifer exclaimed, unable to contain herself. "Cannot you see that you have been spied upon and not simply for a few days. No, more than that. You have been manipulated. I confess to having had a part in that. I wonder if Lord Watching—for I suppose we must call him that—will admit to as much."

"I think he only meant to observe my character," Sir Matthew said in a mild voice, "and I do not think I can blame him for that. As for manipulation, I can see that well enough now. My uncle saw that your cousin would have spelled disaster for me and did no more than what I would have done for him had the circumstances been reversed. As for his more recent attentions to your sister, I can only be relieved that they were not made in earnest. No, more than that. In arousing my jealousy, he brought me to my senses."

Susan cooed with delight and Lady Tassing beamed her approval at this simple speech. But Lord Watching's eyes were on Jennifer and nothing that he saw gave reassurance, for her eyes were blazing with anger.

"No one has asked my opinion, but I will give it all the same!" she declared. "You have all been more understanding by far than this gentleman deserves. He makes the excuse that all has 'come out' well, but that is not thanks to him, I think, for I refuse to believe that such willful deceit is excusable. You all may be willing to think of this gentleman as Sir John Evans who takes his lodgings in a simple house at one moment and as an Earl the next, but I am not!"

"I think you take it all too personally, Jennie!" Susan exclaimed. "If Sir Matthew is willing to understand . . . "

"I am not Sir Matthew!" Jennifer told her. "I, at least, do not take deception lightly. But then, this gentleman has done no more than to demonstrate that he is no better than those members of the *haut ton* whom he pretends to despise. As for me, I have done with this society. In Uncle's present mood he will be glad enough to return to the country. There is Molly's wedding to be thought of as well. And once away from here, I will be able to forget these past weeks. I want no more than that, I assure you. To forget them entirely!"

Chapter Twenty-one

Molly's wedding day was cloudless. For the past two weeks Jennifer had allowed herself to think of nothing except making the necessary bridal arrangements and now it was with some faint sense of satisfaction that she surveyed the garden at Marsden Hall, where a considerable company had gathered to observe the ceremony.

The vicar was already standing in the bower which Jennifer had caused to be covered with roses, and Molly's mother, setting aside her role as cook for the day, was seated with the gentry on one of the gilt chairs which had been removed from the ballroom. She was a stout woman, bravely arrayed in a scarlet gown which matched her complexion and Jennifer saw her begin to dab at her eyes with a handkerchief in happy anticipation as the fiddlers conscripted from the village struck up the wedding march.

Much to everyone's surprise, the Duke of Jennings had claimed the privilege of giving the bride away, and as the guests rose and turned to watch the procession, their gasps were not so much for Molly, lovely in a white gown of Jennifer's design, as for the Duke's unfamiliar smile as he led the bride-to-be down the grassy aisle.

Alfred, having made a belated appearance, struck a pose and, with far more aplomb than Jennifer had seen him display before, held out his hand to the blushing Molly. The fiddlers stopped their music, not quite in unison, and the vicar, a wizened personage of eighty, began to recite the familiar words with a rapidity which demanded the absolute attention of his audience.

So it was that in a shorter time than Jennifer had thought possible the happy couple had plighted their troth and Molly was beaming at the company over Alfred's shoulder. Lord Bemis, apparently unable to contain himself at seeing his footman settled at last, hurried forward to clap the fellow on the back and press something into his hand, which gift Jennifer saw Molly cleverly transfer to her own before it was time for her and the bridegroom to retrace their steps to the unrestrained if not harmonious tune of the fiddles.

Then everyone was hurrying to congratulate the

couple as they took their place close to the tables which were laden with every conceivable delicacy. The excellent wine punch soon gave rise to a certain hilarity which caused the local blacksmith, who no doubt regretted his former perfidy, to kiss Molly soundly, all of which did not distract the bride sufficiently to keep her from preventing the underparlor maid from doing the same to Alfred.

Jennifer found herself beside Lady Tassing, who was heaping a plate high.

"For your uncle, my dear," she explained, nodding her ostrich feather happily. "Does he not look quite a different man? What a relief it is to me to have him safely in the country once more. Why, he has been quite a changed person since Lord Flauntington's apology arrived. And, of course, he has given me the credit for it, as indeed he should. Oh dear, how difficult it is to keep an eye on him today! I declare he must not be allowed to tire himself."

And waving the plate so wildly that much of its contents fell to the grass, she managed to prevent the Duke from bestowing a second kiss on Molly's rosy cheek.

Turning to look about her, Jennifer saw Amelia intent on engaging Lord Bemis in conversation. But although her cousin was at her most animated, it was clear that His Lordship's eyes were on her mother, and Jennifer noted that Lady Daphne seemed more flushed than usual.

"How happily it has all ended," Lady Tassing declared, reappearing with the Duke of Jennings in tow. "And you must congratulate your niece, sir, for it is all her doing."

"The gel looks a bit pale to me," the Duke replied in his usual abrupt manner. "Dose her with tar water tonight. There's the answer."

"Medicine is all very well," Lady Tassing reminded him, "but with Susan soon to be gone, we must be looking to Jennie's future. London is the answer, of course. She must be introduced to society properly. I will see to everything."

"I expect you will," the Duke said with a grimace which did not keep him from glancing at Lady Tassing with a certain fondness.

"I know you only mean to be kind," Jennifer told them, turning very pale. "But I would prefer to see to my own future."

And gathering the blue silk of her gown about her, she hurried away.

Once she was free of the crush, she saw her sister and Sir Matthew in intimate conversation and although, on catching sight of her, they called for her to join them, she murmured some excuse and made her way into the rose garden, where she could be alone.

What a stranger she was to herself now that all of this was over, she thought. For two weeks she had forced herself to think of nothing but Molly's happiness and now that was accomplished, she found herself at a sudden loss. It was, she thought, as though the world had suddenly stopped spinning and she must soon fall off.

She pressed her fingers to her eyes. And at the same moment she heard a voice which she had never again thought to hear but in her dreams softly utter her name. Turning, she saw him standing close to the fountain and, absurdly enough, the first thought to come to her was that he was taller than she remembered him to be.

"What are you doing here, sir?" she cried.

"Would you believe me if I told you that Molly had the goodness to send me an invitation to her wedding?" he replied. "But then, I must be honest. I would have come, if not today, then at some other time and all because you took your leave of me in anger that last morning."

He came toward her slowly, his dark eyes intent on sketching every line of her face as though he sought to memorize it.

"I think that I was wrong to lose my temper, sir," Jennifer said in a low voice. "Indeed, I have given the matter some thought since and I believe that your motives were the best even though the means you chose . . . "

She broke off, finding it strangely difficult to breathe. If only he would not stand so close to her! If only she could find the strength to move away!

"If you will give credit to my motives, I will

agree to fault the means," he told her. "Only assure me that I am not quite despicable."

"I have never called you that, sir!" Jennifer exclaimed.

"Indeed you are too kind to do so."

"Kindness has nothing to do with it!" Jennifer said breathlessly. "You are an honorable gentleman. I have never thought otherwise."

"These words are music to my ears," he said, and although his eyes were still hooded, a smile touched his lips.

"You mock me, sir."

"Ah, that I would never do. I came here for reassurance. Without it my life would remain a misery."

"I declare I cannot believe you," Jennifer replied, her spirit returning. "You have your wealth and your estates. Because of you, your nephew is happily affianced. Misery indeed! I wonder you can speak the word."

"Perhaps you are not familiar with that particular emotion, Miss Damion," he said in a low voice.

"I am more familiar with it than you think," Jennifer told him.

"Is it possible for it to intrude even on this festive occasion?"

"It intrudes everywhere at any time," Jennifer said impulsively.

"Then we understand one another, I think," he murmured. And now his face was very close to hers. In the background the village fiddlers struck up a country tune.

"My dear Jennifer," he said, taking her hand. "Will you believe me when I tell you this is no passing fancy?"

Suddenly Jennifer was caught up on a wave of delight.

"I am in a mood to believe anything you tell me, sir," she declared.

"Then I will tell you that I love you."

"And would you have me say I love you, too?"

"Only if you mean the words."

"I mean them, sir," Jennifer replied, and as the fiddles swelled the tune, she walked into his arms.

THE PASSING BELLS

by

PHILLIP ROCK

A story you'll wish would go on forever.

Here is the vivid story of the Grevilles, a titled British family, and their servants—men and women who knew their place, upstairs and down, until England went to war and the whole fabric of British society began to unravel and change.

"Well-written, exciting. Echoes of Hemingway, Graves and *Upstairs, Downstairs.*"—*Library Journal*

"Every twenty-five years or so, we are blessed with a war novel, outstanding in that it depicts not only the history of a time but also its soul."—*West Coast Review of Books.*

"Vivid and enthralling."—*The Philadelphia Inquirer*

A Dell Book $2.75 (16837-6)

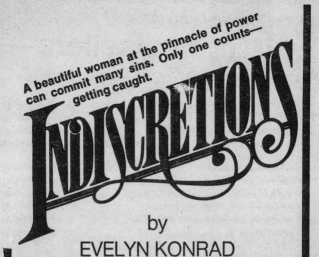

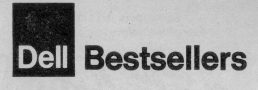
Dell Bestsellers

**Sometimes you have to lose
everything before you can begin**

Author of *The Promise* and
Summer's End

Isabella and Amadeo lived in an elegant
and beautiful world where they shared their
brightest treasure—their boundless, en-
during love. Suddenly, their enchantment
ended and Amadeo vanished forever. With
all her proud courage could she release the
past to embrace her future? Would she ever
dare TO LOVE AGAIN?

A Dell Book $2.50   (18631-5)

At your local bookstore or use this handy coupon for ordering:

SHARON SALVATO
co-author of *The Black Swan*

Bitter Eden

**He taught her what
it means to live
She taught him what it means to love**

Peter Berean rode across the raging
landscape of a countryside in flames.
Callie Dawson, scorched by shame, no
longer believed in love—until she met
Peter's strong, tender gaze. From that
moment they were bound by an unforget-
table promise stronger than his stormy
passions and wilder than her desperate
dreams. Together they would taste the
rich, forbidden fruit of a *Bitter Eden*.

A Dell Book $2.75   (10771-7)